HORRIFYING AND HIDEOUS HAUNTINGS

ALSO EDITED BY HELEN HOKE

A CHILLING COLLECTION

DEMONIC, DANGEROUS AND DEADLY

DEMONS WITHIN

EERIE, WEIRD AND WICKED

GHOSTLY, GRIM AND GRUESOME

MYSTERIOUS, MENACING AND MACABRE

SINISTER, STRANGE AND SUPERNATURAL

SPOOKS, SPOOKS, SPOOKS

TALES OF FEAR AND FRIGHTENING PHENOMENA

TERRORS, TORMENTS AND TRAUMAS

THRILLERS, CHILLERS AND KILLERS

UNCANNY TALES OF UNEARTHLY AND UNEXPECTED HORRORS

VENOMOUS TALES OF VILLAINY AND VENGEANCE

WEIRDIES, WEIRDIES, WEIRDIES

WITCHES, WITCHES, WITCHES

HORRIFYING AND HIDEOUS HAUNTINGS

AN ANTHOLOGY BY
HELEN HOKE
& FRANKLIN HOKE

LODESTAR BOOKS
E. P. DUTTON   NEW YORK

37020000132667

No character in this book is intended to represent any actual person; all the incidents of the stories are entirely fictional in nature.

Copyright © 1986 by Helen Hoke and Franklin Hoke

All rights reserved. No part of this publication may be reproduced or transmitted in any form or by any means, electronic or mechanical, including photocopy, recording, or any information storage and retrieval system now known or to be invented, without permission in writing from the publisher, except by a reviewer who wishes to quote brief passages in connection with a review written for inclusion in a magazine, newspaper, or broadcast.

Library of Congress Cataloging in Publication Data

Horrifying and hideous hauntings.

"Lodestar books."
Contents: Fever dream / Ray Bradbury—The man who didn't believe in ghosts / Nic Leodhas—Dead trouble / Aidan Chambers—[etc.]
 1. Horror tales, American. 2. Horror tales, British. [1. Horror stories. 2. Short stories] I. Hoke, Helen, date. II. Hoke, Franklin.
PZ5.H7627 1986 [Fic] 86-4403
ISBN 0-525-67179-X

Published in the United States by E. P. Dutton, 2 Park Avenue, New York, N.Y. 10016

Published simultaneously in Canada by Fitzhenry & Whiteside Limited, Toronto

Editor: Virginia Buckley

Printed in the U.S.A.   COBE   First Edition
10 9 8 7 6 5 4 3 2 1

ACKNOWLEDGMENTS

The selections in this book are used by permission of and special arrangement with the proprietors of their respective copyrights, who are listed below. The editors' and publisher's thanks go to all who have made this collection possible.

The editors and publisher have made every effort to trace the ownership of all material contained herein. It is their belief that the necessary permissions from publishers, authors, and authorized agents have been obtained in all cases. In the event of any questions arising as to the use of any material, the editors and publisher express regret for any error unconsciously made and will be pleased to make the necessary corrections in future editions of this book.

"The Cyprian Cat," by Dorothy Sayers. From *In the Teeth of the Evidence and 19 Other Stories* by Dorothy Sayers. Copyright © 1943 by Avon Book Company. Copyright renewed 1972 by Anthony Fleming. Reprinted by permission of Watkins Loomis Agency, Inc.

"Dead Trouble," by Aidan Chambers. From *Ghosts 2*. Reprinted by permission of Macmillan, London and Basingstoke.

"Fever Dream," by Ray Bradbury. Reprinted by permission of Don Congdon Associates, Inc. Copyright © 1948 by Ray Bradbury, renewed 1975 by Ray Bradbury.

"Gay As Cheese," by Joan Aiken. From *The Far Forests,* by Joan Aiken. Copyright © Joan Aiken Enterprises, Ltd., 1977. Reprinted by permission of Viking Penguin, Inc.

"The Man Who Didn't Believe in Ghosts," by Sorche Nic Leodhas. From *Ghosts Go Haunting,* by Sorche Nic Leodhas. Copyright © 1965 by Leclaire G. Alger. Reprinted by permission of Holt, Rinehart & Winston, Publishers.

"Meeting in the Park," by Ruth Rendell. Reprinted by permission of the author.

"That Hell-Bound Train," by Robert Bloch. Copyright © 1958 by Mercury Press for the *Magazine of Fantasy and Science Fiction,* September 1958. Reprinted by permission of the author and the author's agents, Scott Meredith Literary Agency, Inc., 845 Third Avenue, New York, New York 10022.

Contents

About This Book / ix

Fever Dream / 1
RAY BRADBURY

The Man Who Didn't Believe in Ghosts / 9
NIC LEODHAS

Dead Trouble / 16
AIDAN CHAMBERS

The Shepherd's Dog / 34
JOYCE MARSH

Meeting in the Park / 48
RUTH RENDELL

The Cyprian Cat / 62
DOROTHY SAYERS

A Haunted Island / 76
ALGERNON BLACKWOOD

Gay As Cheese / 94
JOAN AIKEN

That Hell-Bound Train / 100
ROBERT BLOCH

ABOUT THIS BOOK

THE KNOWN WORLD IS VAST, but there is another world about which we know little, and it is to the edge of this fearsome realm we invite our readers to venture. Beyond this border lurk the sinister and terrifying. It is the province of weird inhabitants and the spawning ground of our nightmares. It is a land into which the more timorous traveler will enter with the chill of fright.

What is this realm of shadows and fear? Some call it death. Hamlet called it "the undiscovered country from whose bourn no traveler returns." Each of these writers takes his own path through this realm of darkness. All find the road a bit treacherous.

In Ray Bradbury's "Fever Dream," the doctor patiently explains to a young boy named Charles that he has come down with a fever, nothing too serious. But the boy is certain that something much worse is happening to him. A mere "fever dream," the doctor concludes about the boy's worries. But in the end, it's difficult to be sure just what *has* become of Charles.

"The Man Who Didn't Believe in Ghosts" is Nic Leodhas's whimsical tale of a young skeptic stubbornly ignoring the ghost of a beautiful maiden in his home. She is persistent, though, and

ABOUT THIS BOOK

finally he must resort to some romantic matchmaking in the other world to put her soul to rest.

Pity the poor young ghost in Aidan Chambers' "Dead Trouble." Try as he might to communicate with the living, he just can't seem to get it right. But with considerable advice from the older spooks, and plenty of energy and imagination on his part, he continues to try!

The bond between a shepherd and his faithful dog is stronger than anyone suspects in Joyce Marsh's "The Shepherd's Dog." Unable at first to know what his duty should be after the death of his Master, the loyal dog, Chauval, is finally able to answer the Master's call.

"Meeting in the Park," by Ruth Rendell, is a story of love and of what is called the double, or counterpart, of a living person. It seems that Peter develops some confusion concerning the mirror image of his girl, Lisa . . . confusion that proves deadly.

In "The Cyprian Cat," by Dorothy Sayers, a man whose only true crime is a deep loathing of cats finds himself on trial for a murder surrounded by highly unusual, incriminating circumstances. Only the giant Cyprian cat that steals into his room on the night of the killing, much to his fright, can know, if not tell, the full truth.

Truly bloodcurdling, Algernon Blackwood's "A Haunted Island" is the account of a man isolated on an island in the lake country of Canada, reading for his law examinations. The silence deepens as his days pass in solitary study, until two spectral beings move with determined purpose into the young student's life. Here again, the double brings chilling horror to the tale.

In "Gay As Cheese," by Joan Aiken, a barber, cheerful Mr. Pol, has the unusual ability to know every detail of a customer's life, from his birth to his death, merely by laying his hands upon the man's head before trimming his hair. But when a young couple drops by for his services, Mr. Pol learns more than he would have liked about their future.

Always the master of the haunting tale, Robert Bloch is the

About This Book

natural choice to bring these travels to a close with "That Hell-Bound Train." Martin strikes a deal with the Devil and, while the Devil is always a hard bargainer, Martin wonders if he might not have gotten the better of the deal.

These excursions into the undiscovered country are some of the finest work these writers have done; we think you will enjoy them as much as we did.

Helen Hoke

Franklin Hoke

Fever Dream

RAY BRADBURY

They put him between fresh, clean, laundered sheets and there was always a newly squeezed glass of thick orange juice on the table under the dim pink lamp. All Charles had to do was call and Mom or Dad would stick their heads into his room to see how sick he was. The acoustics of the room were fine; you could hear the toilet gargling its porcelain throat in the mornings, you could hear rain tap the roof or sly mice run in the secret walls, the canary singing in its cage downstairs. If you were very alert, sickness wasn't too bad.

He was fifteen, Charles was. It was mid-September, with the land beginning to burn with autumn. He lay in the bed for three days before the terror overcame him.

His hand began to change. His right hand. He looked at it and it was hot and sweating there on the comforter, alone. It moved a bit, fluttering. Then it lay there, changing color.

That afternoon the doctor came again and tapped his thin chest like a little drum. "How are you?" asked the doctor, smiling. "I know, don't tell me: 'My *cold* is fine, Doctor, but I feel lousy!' Ha!" He laughed at his own oft-repeated joke.

Charles lay there and for him that terrible and ancient jest was becoming a reality. The joke fixed itself in his mind. His mind touched and drew away from it in a pale terror. The doctor did not know how cruel he was with his jokes! "Doctor," whispered Charles, lying flat and colorless. "My *hand,* it doesn't *belong* to me anymore. This morning it *changed* into something else. I want you to change it back, Doctor. Doctor!"

The doctor showed his teeth and patted his hand. "It looks fine to me, son. You just had a little fever dream."

"But it changed, Doctor. Oh, Doctor," cried Charles, pitifully holding up his pale wild hand. "It *did*!"

The doctor winked. "I'll give you a pink pill for that." He popped a tablet onto Charles's tongue. "Swallow!"

"Will it make my hand change back and become *me,* again?"

"Yes, yes."

The house was silent when the doctor drove off down the road in his carriage under the quiet, blue September sky. A clock ticked far below in the kitchen world. Charles lay looking at his hand.

It did not change back. It was still—something else.

The wind blew outside. Leaves fell against the cool window.

At four o'clock his other hand changed. It seemed almost to become a fever, a chemical, a virus. It pulsed and shifted, cell by cell. It beat like a warm heart. The fingernails turned blue and then red. It took about an hour for it to change and when it was finished, it looked just like any ordinary hand. But it was not ordinary. It no longer was his anymore. He lay in a fascinated horror and then fell into an exhausted sleep.

Mother brought the soup up at six. He wouldn't touch it. "I haven't any hands," he said, eyes shut.

"Your hands are perfectly good," said Mother.

"No," he wailed. "My hands are gone. I feel like I have stumps. Oh, Mama, Mama, hold me, hold me. I'm scared!"

She had to feed him herself.

"Mama," he said, "get the doctor, please, again. I'm so sick."

"The doctor'll be here tonight at eight," she said, and went out.

Fever Dream

At seven, with night dark and close around the house, Charles was sitting up in bed when he felt the thing happening to first one leg, then the other. "Mama! Come quick!" he screamed.

But when Mama came, the thing was no longer happening.

When she went downstairs, he simply lay without fighting as his legs beat and beat, grew warm, red-hot, and the room filled with the warmth of his feverish change. The glow crept up from his toes to his ankles and then to his knees.

"May I come in?" The doctor smiled in the doorway.

"Doctor!" cried Charles. "Hurry, take off my blankets!"

The doctor lifted the blankets tolerantly. "There you are. Whole and healthy. Sweating, though. A little fever. I told you not to move around, bad boy." He pinched the moist pink cheek. "Did the pills help? Did your hand change back?"

"No, no, now it's my other hand and my legs!"

"Well, well, I'll have to give you three more pills, one for each limb, eh, my little peach?" laughed the doctor.

"Will they help me? Please, please. What've I *got*?"

"A mild case of scarlet fever, complicated by a slight cold."

"Is it a germ that lives and has more little germs in me?"

"Yes."

"Are you *sure* it's scarlet fever? You haven't taken any tests!"

"I guess I know a certain fever when I see one," said the doctor, checking the boy's pulse with cool authority.

Charles lay there, not speaking until the doctor was crisply packing his black kit. Then in the silent room, the boy's voice made a small, weak pattern, his eyes alight with remembrance. "I read a book once. About petrified trees, wood turning to stone. About how trees fell and rotted and minerals got in and built up and they look just like trees, but they're not, they're stone." He stopped. In the quiet, warm room his breathing sounded.

"Well?" asked the doctor.

"I've been thinking," said Charles after a time. "Do germs ever get big? I mean, in biology class they told us about one-celled animals, amoebas and things, and how, millions of years

[3]

ago, they got together until there was a bunch and they made the first body. And more and more cells got together and got bigger and then finally maybe there was a fish and finally here *we* are, and all we are is a bunch of cells that decided to get together, to help each other out. Isn't that right?" Charles wet his feverish lips.

"What's all this about?" The doctor bent over him.

"I've got to tell you this. Doctor, oh, I've *got* to!" he cried. "What would happen, oh just pretend, please pretend, that just like in the old days, a lot of microbes got together and wanted to make a bunch, and reproduced and made *more*—"

His white hands were on his chest now, crawling toward his throat.

"And they decided to *take over* a person!" cried Charles.

"Take over a person?"

"Yes, *become* a person. *Me,* my hands, my feet! What if a disease somehow knew how to kill a person and yet live after him?"

He screamed.

The hands were on his neck.

The doctor moved forward, shouting.

At nine o'clock the doctor was escorted out to his carriage by the mother and father, who handed him up his bag. They conversed in the cool night wind for a few minutes. "Just be sure his hands are kept strapped to his legs," said the doctor. "I don't want him hurting himself!"

"Will he be all right, Doctor?" The mother held to his arm a moment.

He patted her shoulder. "Haven't I been your family physician for thirty years? It's the fever, he imagines things."

"But those bruises on his throat—he almost choked himself."

"Just you keep him strapped; he'll be all right in the morning."

The horse and carriage moved off down the dark September road.

Fever Dream

At three in the morning, Charles was still awake in his small back room. The bed was damp under his head and his back. He was very warm. Now he no longer had any arms or legs, and his body was beginning to change. He did not move on the bed, but looked at the vast blank ceiling space with insane concentration. For a while he had screamed and thrashed, but now he was weak and hoarse from it, and his mother had gotten up a number of times to soothe his brow with a wet towel. Now he was silent, his hands strapped to his legs.

He felt the walls of his body change, the organs shift, the lungs catch fire like burning bellows of pink alcohol. The room was lighted up as with the flickerings of a hearthplace.

Now he had no body. It was all gone. It was under him, but it was filled with a vast pulse of some burning, lethargic drug. It was as if a guillotine had neatly lopped off his head and his head lay shining on a midnight pillow while the body, below, still alive, belonged to somebody else. The disease had eaten his body and from the eating had reproduced itself in feverish duplicate. There were the little hand hairs and the fingernails and the scars and the toenails and the tiny mole on his right hip, all done again in perfect fashion.

I am dead, he thought. I've been killed, and yet I live. My body is dead, it is all disease and nobody will know. I will walk around and it will not be me, it will be something else. It will be something all bad, all evil, so big and so evil it's hard to understand or think about. Something that will buy shoes and drink water and get married someday maybe and do more evil in the world than has ever been done.

Now the warmth was stealing up his neck, into his cheeks, like a hot wine. His lips burned; his eyelids, like leaves, caught fire. His nostrils breathed out blue flame, faintly, faintly.

This will be all, he thought. It'll take my head and my brain and fix each eye and every tooth and all the marks in my brain, and every hair and every wrinkle in my ears, and there'll be nothing left of *me*.

He felt his brain fill with a boiling mercury. He felt his left eye clench in upon itself and, like a snail, withdraw, shift. He was blind in his left eye. It no longer belonged to him. It was enemy territory. His tongue was gone, cut out. His left cheek was numbed, lost. His left ear stopped hearing. It belonged to someone else now. This thing that was being born, this mineral thing replacing the wooden log, this disease replacing healthy animal cells.

He tried to scream and he was able to scream loud and high and sharply in the room, just as his brain flooded down, his right eye and right ear were cut out; he was blind and deaf, all fire and terror, all panic, all death.

His scream stopped before his mother ran through the door to his side.

It was a good, clear morning, with a brisk wind that helped carry doctor, horse, and carriage along the road to halt before the house. In the window above, the boy stood, fully dressed. He did not wave when the doctor waved and called, "What's this? Up? My God!"

The doctor almost ran upstairs. He came gasping into the bedroom.

"What are you doing out of bed?" he demanded of the boy. He tapped his thin chest, took his pulse and temperature. "Absolutely amazing! Normal. Normal, by God!"

"I shall never be sick again in my life," declared the boy, quietly, standing there, looking out of the wide window. "Never."

"I hope not. Why, you're looking fine, Charles."

"Doctor?"

"Yes, Charles?"

"Can I go to school *now*?" asked Charles.

"Tomorrow will be time enough. You sound positively eager."

"I am. I like school. All the kids. I want to play with them and wrestle with them, and spit on them and play with the girls' pigtails and shake the teacher's hand, and rub my hands on all the cloaks in the cloakroom, and I want to grow up and travel and shake hands with people all over the world, and be married and have lots of children, and go to libraries and handle books and—*all* of that. I want to!" said the boy, looking off into the September morning. "What's the name you call me?"

"What?" The doctor puzzled. "I called you nothing but Charles."

"It's better than no name at all, I guess." Charles shrugged.

"I'm glad you want to go back to school," said the doctor.

"I really anticipate it," smiled the boy. "Thank you for your help, Doctor. Shake hands."

"Glad to."

They shook hands gravely, and the clear wind blew through the open window. They shook hands for almost a minute, the boy smiling up at the old man and thanking him.

Then, laughing, the boy raced the doctor downstairs and out to his carriage. His mother and father followed for the happy farewell.

"Fit as a fiddle!" said the doctor. "Incredible!"

"And strong," said the father. "He got out of his straps himself during the night. Didn't you, Charles?"

"Did I?" said the boy.

"You did! How?"

"Oh," the boy said, "that was a long time ago."

"A long time ago!"

They all laughed, and while they were laughing, the quiet boy moved his bare foot on the pavement and brushed against a number of red ants that were scurrying about on the pavement. Secretly, his eyes shining, while his parents chatted with the old man, he saw the ants hesitate, quiver, and lie still on the cement. He knew they were cold now.

"Good-bye!"

The doctor drove away, waving.

The boy walked ahead of his parents. As he walked, he looked away toward the town and began to hum "School Days" under his breath.

"It's good to have him well again," said the father.

"Listen to him. He's so looking forward to school!"

The boy turned quietly. He gave each of his parents a crushing hug. He kissed them both several times.

Then, without a word, he bounded up the steps into the house.

In the parlor, before the others entered, he quickly opened the birdcage, thrust his hand in, and petted the yellow canary, *once*.

Then he shut the cage door, stood back, and waited.

The Man Who Didn't Believe in Ghosts

NIC LEODHAS

IN A TOWN NOT FAR FROM EDINBURGH, there was a house that was said to be haunted. It wasn't the sort of house you'd think would attract a ghost at all. It was only a two-story cottage with a garret, and it was far too neat and pretty for ghosts to care much about. The outside walls of it were painted white and its casement windows had diamond-shaped panes to them. There was a climbing rose trained over the front door, and there was a flower garden before the house and a kitchen garden behind it, with a pear tree and an apple tree and a small green lawn. Who'd ever think that a ghost could choose to bide in a place like that? But folks did say it was haunted, all the same.

The house had belonged to an old attorney with only one child, a daughter. Folks old enough to remember her still say that there never was another lass as bonny as her in the town. The old man loved her dearly but she died early. There was an old sad story told about her being in love with the son of an old laird who did not favor the match. The poor lad died of a fever while they were still courting, and not long after, she died too—folks said of a broken heart.

After that the old man lived alone in the house, with a woman coming in each day to take care of it. There wasn't a word said about ghosts in the old man's time. He'd not have put up with it for a minute.

When the old attorney died, there was nobody left that was kin to him but a second cousin several times removed. So to keep the property in the family, the old man left all he had to the cousin, including the house, of course.

The young man was grateful, but as he was not married, he had little use for a house. The lodgings he was living in suited him fine. So he put the renting of the house into an agent's hands. The rent money would make a nice little nest egg against the time when he decided he would like to get married. When that time came, he'd want the house for himself.

It was the folks the agent found to live in the house that started all the talk about ghosts. At first they were very well pleased with the house, but as time passed they began to notice queer things were happening in it. Doors would open and close again, with nobody at all near them. When the young wife was dusting the spare bedroom, she heard drawers being pulled open and shut again behind her, but when she turned about to look, no one at all was there.

Things were lifted and put down again before the tenants very eyes, but they couldn't see who was lifting them or putting them down. They came to have the feeling that there was somebody always in the house with them. Of course, they tried to be sensible about it, but it gave them a terrible eerie feeling. As for getting a maid to stay, it couldn't be done! The maids all said that they felt that someone was always looking over their shoulders while they worked, and every time they set something down, it got itself moved to another place. They wouldn't take it upon themselves to say why, but they'd take whatever pay was coming to them, and go. And they did.

The end of the tenants' stay in the house came upon the day when the young wife came into the sitting room to find her wee lad rolling his ball across the floor. Every time the ball reached the middle of the room, it seemed to turn and roll itself back to him, as if someone who couldn't be seen were playing with him. But when he looked up at his mother and laughed and said "Bonny lady!" 'twas more than she could bear. She caught him up in her arms and ran out of the door to one of the neighbors, and no one could persuade her to set foot in the house again. So her husband went to the agent and told him they were sorry, but the way things were, they'd have to give up the house.

The young man to whom the house had been left was a very matter-of-fact young fellow. He didn't believe in ghosts. He was quite put out because the story had got around that there were ghosts in the house. Of course, the young couple who had lived there couldn't be depended on not to talk about what had happened. It wouldn't have been according to human nature for them to keep quiet about it. What made it awkward was that by this time the young man had found a lass he wanted to marry, but unfortunately she had heard the story. And she *did* believe in ghosts.

She said that she loved him dearly and would like very much to marry him. But she told him flatly that she could never, *never* bring herself to live in a haunted house.

Well, the doors did open and close of themselves, but that didn't daunt him. He just took them off their hinges and rehung them. They went on opening and closing just the same, but he said that was only because of a flaw in the walls.

He had to admit to himself that he heard drawers opening and closing, and latches of cupboards clicking shut. There was a tinkling in the china closet, too, as if someone were moving the cups and plates about. And once or twice he thought he heard water running in the scullery. But when he looked, every tap was shut off tight. Besides, he knew there was no one but himself in the house. So he said that old houses were always full of queer noises because of the foundations settling, and paid them no more heed.

Even when a book he had just closed and laid on the table opened itself again, and the leaves turned over slowly as if someone were looking at them, he told himself that it was just a puff of wind from the window did it, although afterward he remembered that the windows were closed at the time.

But still he didn't believe in ghosts.

So he went on living in the house and trying to persuade his sweetheart to marry him and come and live there with him. And, of course, to convince her that the house wasn't haunted at all. But he had no luck, for she wouldn't be persuaded.

Well, things went on in this unsatisfactory way until his summer holidays came around. He decided, now that he had the time for it, to do something he'd been meaning to do and never got around to. There were a lot of clothes in the attic that had belonged to the old lawyer and his daughter. It seemed sinful to leave them there to moulder away when some poor body'd be glad to have them. So what he was going to do was to pack them all up and send them to the Missionary Society, where a good use would be found for them.

He went up to the garret and found some empty boxes, and began to pack the clothes. They were all hanging in several tall wardrobes, ranged around the room. He packed the old lawyer's clothes first. There were a good many of them, suits and coats and boots and shoes, all of the best quality, to say nothing of a quantity of warm underclothing in boxes neatly stacked on the floors of the wardrobes. When he had taken everything out and folded it neatly, he packed the boxes and set them out of his way, and turned to the wardrobe that held the dead lass's clothes. When he opened the first wardrobe, there was a sound uncommonly like a sigh. It gave him a start for a moment, but then he laughed and told himself that it was only the silk of garments brushing against each other in the breeze made by the opening door. He began to take them out, one by one, and to fold them and gently lay them in the box he'd set ready for them. It made him feel a little bit sad and sentimental to be handling the dresses that had been worn by the pretty young thing who had died so young and so long ago.

He'd laid away five or six of them when he came to one frock that seemed strangely heavy for the material of which it was made. It was a light, crisp cotton sprigged with flowers still bright in spite of the years it had hung in the wardrobe. He thought that a dress like that should have had almost no weight at all, so he looked it over curiously. Perhaps a brooch or a buckle was the answer? Then he found a pocket set in the seam of the skirt, and in the pocket a small red book and a letter. It was a letter of the old style, with no envelope, and the dead girl's name and address on the outer folded sheet. He laid the dress aside and, taking his find to the low-set window, he sat down on the floor to read what he had found. He was not a man to read other people's letters and secrets, but something made him feel that it was right to do so now.

He read the letter first. It said:

My dear love:
 Although they have not told me, I know that I am very ill. It may be that we shall not meet again in this world. If I should die, I beg of you to make them promise that when you, too, are dead, we shall lie together side by side.
 Your true love

The young man sat for a while, thinking of the letter, wondering how it had come to the lass, remembering that he had heard that the old laird was dead set against the match. Then he took up the little red book and opened it. The little book was a sort of day-by-day diary with the date printed at the top of each page. It had begun as a sort of housekeeping journal. There was a lot in it about household affairs. There were records of sewing done, of jars of pickles and jams laid by, and about the house being turned out and cleaned from end to end, and such things. But through it all was the story of a young girl's heart. She told about meeting the laird's son, where they first met and when he first spoke to her of love and what they said and how they planned to marry as soon as the old laird could be persuaded to give his consent to the match. Although he was against it, they thought he might be brought over in time.

But they had no time, poor young things! Soon after, the diary told of the letter that John the Carrier had brought her, that had frightened her terribly. And the next page said only, "My love is dead." Page after page was empty after that. Then toward the end of the little book she had written: "I know that I am going to die. I asked my father today to promise to beg the laird to let me lie beside my love when I am dead, but he only turned away and would not answer. I am afraid his pride will not let him ask a favor of one who would not accept me into his family. But, oh my love, if he does not, I'll find a way to bring things right. I'll never rest until I do."

And that was all.

The young man raised his eyes from the page and repeated thoughtfully, "I'll never rest until I do."

It was right then and there that he began to believe in ghosts!

He put the diary and the letter into his pocket, and leaving everything just as it was in the garret, he went downstairs. The packing could wait for another day. He had something better to do. As he went, he thought of the old attorney living there day after day with the ghost of his dead daughter mutely beseeching him to do what his pride would never let him do.

"Well, I have no pride at all," the young man said.

He packed a bag and put on his hat and coat, and started for the station. But as he went out the door, he turned and put his head back in and called out, "Do not fret yourself any longer, lass! You can rest now. I'll find the way to bring things right."

At the station he was fortunate enough to find a train that would take him where he wanted to go. When he got off the train, he asked about the village for news of the laird. Och, the old laird was long dead, folks told him, and a rare old curmudgeon that one was, though they shouldn't be saying it of the dead. But the new laird, him that was the old laird's nephew, had the estate now, and a finer man you'd not be finding should you search for a year and a day.

So up to the castle the young man went. When he got there he found the new laird as reasonable a man as he could hope to

The Man Who Didn't Believe in Ghosts

find. So he gave him the letter and the diary and let him read the story for himself. Then he told him about his house and the ghost in it that would not rest until she had her way.

The old laird's nephew listened gravely, and at the end of the young man's story he sighed and said, "Fifty years! Fifty long years! What a weary time to wait. Poor lass."

The old laird's nephew believed in ghosts himself.

He called his solicitors at once and got them to work. They were so quick about it that by the time the young man got back home after paying a visit to the old laird's nephew who asked him to stay till all was settled, the two lovers were reunited at last and lay together side by side in the old laird's family tomb.

When he got home, he could tell the minute he stepped through the door that there was no one there but himself. There was no more trouble with the doors, and the only sounds were the ordinary sounds that he made himself.

He finally persuaded the lass he wanted to marry to come for supper one night and bring along the old aunt she lived with. The aunt prided herself on having such a keen scent for ghosts that she could actually smell one if it was in a house. So they came, and as soon as they were all settled at the supper table, the aunt looked all around the room and sniffed two or three times.

"Ghosts? Nonsense, my dear!" she said to the young man's lass firmly. "There isn't a single ghost in this house. You may be sure I'd know at once if there were!"

That satisfied the young lady. So, soon she and the young man were married. They lived together so happily in the house that folks completely forgot that it had ever been said that it was haunted. It didn't look at all like the kind of a house that would ever have a ghost. Only the young man remembered.

He really *did* believe in ghosts, after all.

Dead Trouble

AIDAN CHAMBERS

THE TROUBLE WITH BEING DEAD is that no one believes you are alive. Things were different years ago. Or so I'm told by others better able to know than myself. In earlier times people still believed in God and the Devil, and therefore, of course, in ghosts. But nowadays all that has changed.

Only last week, for instance, one of the oldest inhabitants in these parts made a chilling appearance at a party where the guests were playing on the Ouija board. But instead of being received with shocked horror, he was laughed at. Imagine it! The guests laughed and said he wasn't there at all, that they had all had too much to drink, which, along with the Ouija, had affected their imaginations, making them *think* they saw a ghost. My own experiences in the last few months, since I was forced to take up this way of life, have been pretty humiliating, but this treatment of an expert, senior ghost, a professional you might say, was a scandal. People here talked about it for days, and the poor fellow himself was so upset he spent every night for weeks afterward lying around sulking invisibly. And I don't blame him; the whole business was dispiriting.

But I'd better begin at the beginning, otherwise I'll never get to the purpose of this message:

Dead Trouble

Three months ago I fell into the concrete mixer at work. The mixer was a huge affair, not one of those little ones you see churning away on small building sites. We made bulk concrete in it, ready for transporting in large quantities by truck to major constructions. At any rate, I fell in. I blame myself, really; it was no one else's fault. I should have kept my mind on my work instead of thinking about Veronica. (She was my girlfriend at the time, and was being a bit troublesome.)

Before I go on, I must explain that death is quite different viewed from my present situation than it is viewed from yours. As with most things in life—or after it, come to that—death does not seem half so bad when it is all over as you think it is going to be before it happens. Just like going to the dentist is worse to think about beforehand than it is when you get there, and is often quite a laugh afterward. Well, dying is just the same; we here are always laughing about it, especially when people have just arrived—it is such a relief to them, and they wonder what all the fuss was about.

Like so many "modern" people, I used to think death meant the end of everything. Kaput. The finish. Needless to say, I know differently now. (Mind you, there have been times during the last few months when I have wished my death really *had* been the end!)

Death is like everything else in another way too. Some people die lucky; others don't. I didn't. Though up till my death I had been pretty fortunate, the episode with the concrete mixer seemed to change all that. I haven't had a stroke of luck since.

Let me explain.

When I slipped into the mixer, I was on my own. My mate Harry was having his tea break; I was keeping things going until he returned to relieve me. But when he got back, I had gone. He isn't particularly bright, isn't Harry, and he didn't think of looking in the mixer for me. He thought I'd gone off sick.

At home, my family (father, mother, sister) started worrying when I didn't get in that night. But they waited until the following morning, then they informed the police. After a bit of investigating, everyone decided I must have run off, and the police put me on the missing persons list.

Meanwhile, of course, I had been churning around with the half-mixed concrete. I hadn't expected to fall in, so I escaped the awful business of knowing I was going to die, though as it turned out, it wasn't such an ordeal as you might suppose. For a start, it was over quickly. A slip of the foot, a nasty couple of minutes swilling about with the sand and gravel and cement and water, and I was dead. (I didn't much care for the gravel—I've always had a fairly sensitive skin—but the change of state from what I was to what I am now happened in the blink of an eye, and was really rather a pleasant sensation. Like sliding into sleep.)

My death having happened, I was in a position to watch developments without feeling a thing. Or, to put it more accurately, without feeling anything that was being done to my "mortal remains," my corpse.

When Harry got back from his tea break, he transferred the load of mixed concrete into a truck, and, as my remains were by then well mixed with the concrete, they were transferred to the truck too. The truck drove off to a building site in central Manchester, and there the load of concrete (and my corpse) was poured straight into a mold for a stanchion that was to be used as one of the main supports of the building.

And there my remains remain, cased in concrete, fifty feet above ground, and now quite solid. (As one of my less tasteful companions here put it, a rather stiff stiff. I did not reward his unseemly remark with even the ghost of a smile.)

Being sealed in a pillar of concrete, however, is the cause of the trouble I now find myself in. For, unfortunately, no one knows my earthly remains are there. No one, that is, who hasn't yet died. Worse still, no one knows *I'm* dead. Which is why my spiritual being is trapped here in this ghostly condition. As far as I can gather, one of the reasons, among many, why people get stuck between "life" and "afterlife" is that their deaths are unknown to their earthbound relatives.

Dead Trouble

(I was very surprised, I might tell you, to discover how many people get caught in this state of being, for all kinds of reasons. You expect to find murderers, of course, and there are plenty—though on the whole they turn out to be jolly nice blokes; but I was taken aback at the number of schoolteachers, for example, and politicians, and army officers. The teachers and politicians spend most of their time trying to talk their way out into the "afterlife," and never succeed. The army officers, however, take to this life very well. They enjoy going on what they call "chill jaunts"—the kind of haunting that makes earthbound people scream and turn pale. I need hardly add they do this as badly as most of them did everything else in their earth life. Not that this matters much, for with its loss of popularity among earth people, ghostly haunting is rather a disappointing occupation these days. Everybody here is in very low spirits about it.)

But I'm rambling again. It's one of the hazards of being a ghost. You have so much time on your hands and very little to do with it.

As I say, being caught in the in-between, ghostly life—a kind of limbo-land between mortality and eternity—is a bit of a bore, and my aim is to pass on as quickly as possible. But to do this, my relatives must be informed of my death. And as they are not likely to discover my remains in their present secure location, the chances of my parents discovering my death are pretty slim. So I decided I must somehow or other get a message to them.

You have no idea how difficult it is to get a simple message from the "dead" to the "living"! The living just won't listen, and this present climate of disbelief in the afterlife only makes the task more difficult. I asked some of the older ghosts around here for advice. Everyone told me the same thing: Don't bother. It would be a waste of time and energy, they said, and I'd only end up getting the jitters. I know now what they meant: Talking to people who pretend you aren't there is worse than being banished. At least when people send you away, they don't pretend you aren't there; they just ignore you.

However, being a newcomer to the ghostly life, I refused to listen to such good advice. They were all old codgers, I told myself, spirits whose energies were worn out, sapped by years of failure. They had stopped trying ("given up the ghost" seemed hardly the right expression under the circumstances). What was wanted was a little enterprise, a little originality, and most of all, some determination. I believed I possessed all three in quantity. My older companions smiled tolerantly, as wise old men always do when confronted with youthful foolishness, and drifted away to enjoy themselves at their leisure.

So, heedless to good counsel, I set to work. Two factors led to my first method of attempting to get in touch. First, though I wanted to communicate with my relatives, I did not want to upset them by suddenly materializing unannounced in the front room at home while they were watching television. They might have joined me in my present state, dispatched here by shock. Dad, after all, has a weak heart, and Mum has always been of a nervous disposition. I did think of contacting my girlfriend Veronica, who, in a way, was responsible for the situation I am now in. But she had already taken up with another fellow, and the one thing that was clear to me even then was that it is useless trying to make contact with mortals who have lost all interest in you, as well as having no belief in ghosts anyway. Veronica had certainly lost interest in me within a couple of days of my "disappearance," as I knew from what I had observed of her evenings out with her new boyfriend (the one who was causing the trouble that started me thinking that led to me slipping into the concrete mixer!). As for ghosts—Veronica went all through the film of *Nightmare House* without a twinge of fear, while it scared me for weeks. So Veronica was out!

The second thing that decided me on my first course of action was that, being a novice at materialization and ghostly activities in general, it was easier to appear at the place of my death than anywhere else. That meant a haunting of the mixing yard at work.

Dead Trouble

Fine, I thought, just right. I'll do my stuff in front of Harry, and I'll appear looking just as I did on the fatal day, dressed in my overalls. He'd be sure to recognize me then, and be less likely to get the willies, thinking he is seeing any old ghost.

With the confidence that ignorance inspires in men, I went through the materialization routine and successfully took my former shape three feet from Harry at four thirty on the afternoon of the Thursday following the day I died. It was a beautiful day, the sun shining from a blue sky as it sank toward the spring evening. Harry was tending the mixer stripped down to his vest he was so warm.

I stood there in front of him for a full minute and more, waiting for him to catch sight of me. I nodded and smiled in a friendly way so that he would know I wasn't a malevolent type (we had, after all, had our arguments from time to time). He kept glancing at me, but showed not a flicker of reaction. At first this didn't bother me; he's a slow-witted lad. But then I started to lose patience. I waved at him, danced about a bit, even took a step nearer to him. He would have to be blind not to see me now, I thought.

Then I heard a cough at my elbow. I dematerialized to find an old ghost by the name of Cathcart Fitzgammon standing by my side. He was tut-tutting in a haughty manner, and shaking the gray-haired locks he insists on keeping so as to retain his eighteenth-century looks.

"Dash it, young feller," he said. "You'll do no good like that."

I felt a bit bad-tempered that he had interrupted my very first haunt in such a way.

"Why not?" I snapped.

"Daylight haunts need considerable skill and experience, old chap," he said. "Besides which, you were standing with the setting sun right behind you. That poor mortal whose attention you hoped to attract would never have seen you, no matter how bright you managed to make your appearance. You haven't a hope in . . . er . . . on Earth of catching his eye. If I were you I'd have a go during the night. It's easier then."

He drifted off without another word, chuckling to himself.

Of course, I had to admit that Cathcart was right. He had also put me off my stroke, and I needed time to collect myself again. So I postponed operations for an hour or two while I considered the situation.

The difficulty was that if I appeared in daylight Harry would probably not see me, but if I waited until dark, or dusk even, Harry would have gone home, so that there would be no one to communicate with anyhow, and I'd be left shivering and alone in the cold.

As far as I could see, there was only one solution. I found Harry's car in the work's parking lot, dissolved inside, and made myself comfortable on the backseat, intending to wait until Harry knocked off work and went home. Then, when he went out for the evening, I'd materialize on the passenger seat beside him at a convenient moment and tell him my news. That way I'd know where Harry was when darkness fell, saving myself ohms of energy flying about looking for him.

Parking lots are dismal places, as much for ghosts as mortals —which is why you rarely hear of hauntings in them—and there was no one about of my kind to pass the time of day with; so very soon I was bored, and what with the bright sun and the stuffy warmth of Harry's car, I very soon dozed off. (There's nothing like bright light and warmth for setting a ghost nodding.) Half an hour after dissolving into Harry's car, I was as dormant as a flat battery.

I came to hours later. Night had fallen, and was encouragingly black, without the stars or moon. It was so black, I thought at first the car must be parked in Harry's garage. But then I heard a noise from the front seat that indicated very clearly that we weren't in Harry's garage at all. I looked up and there was Harry, necking with his girlfriend, a shapely lass from the accounts office at work. We were parked under some trees in a picnic area just out of town.

Dead Trouble

Naturally, I felt a little uncomfortable. I'm not one of those ghosts who go around peeping at friends they've left behind, enjoying the sight of them in all kinds of situations both public and private. (Personally, I think that's as sick an occupation for a ghost as it is for a mortal.) But I'd spent a good deal of time and energy already keeping up with Harry so that I could get my message to him, and I wasn't going to give in now.

I had to act quickly, before things got really embarrassing. Without another thought I went through the drill for materialization at double-quick pace. Unfortunately, in my haste I put too much energy into some parts of the drill and not enough into others, and was rather careless overall. My lack of experience as a haunter, you see! The result was astonishing and, but for the circumstances, might have been both interesting and amusing.

The materialization got completely out of control. Instead of appearing as myself in a gentle glow of unearthly light, I came out as a collection of very violent, phosphorescent colors revealing a hideous object with an enormous head, twisted features, a bloated body, and unfinished, stunted arms and legs.

I did not realize at first just how I looked, for, of course, my attention was fully directed at Harry's back so that I should be ready to speak soothing words as soon as he turned around. So, thinking all was well, I coughed politely to attract his attention. But the cough also came out quite unlike what I intended. Instead of a soft, hacking noise, I heard myself produce what I can only describe as a torrent of prolonged and vicious snarls.

At once I knew that something was wrong, took a glance at myself, and immediately felt angry with myself for being so careless. Which only made matters worse. For my annoyance was transmitted into the materialization and imprinted itself on the warped features of the ghostly figure I had projected, turning an already ghastly face into something so horrible that I almost fainted at the sight of it.

The blaze of phosphor colors, the appearance of my misshapen ghost, the imprinting of my anger on its features: All happened in the blinking of an eye. But it was enough to attract Harry's and his girl's attention. They unraveled themselves with incredible speed, swung around in their seats, and came face to face with my apparition just as the snarls that were meant to be a cough broke the silence of the night.

For a split second they stared in wide-eyed disbelief at the appalling creature hovering in the air above the backseat. Stunned shock was replaced by nerve-shattered fear. The blood drained from their faces; their mouths dropped open. Then each one let out a hysterical scream.

This brought me to my senses. I dematerialized with such speed that the warped and shining figure I had created, instead of fading away exploded like a searchlight bulb fusing from a short circuit. The car was plunged into a blackness that seemed, by contrast with the brief brilliance of my ghostly glow, to be tangible.

I had no time to think how I might remedy my awful error. Harry's girl flung open the car door and ran in blind terror, screaming into the night. Harry was only a heartbeat behind.

They left me exhausted on the backseat.

It took me an hour to collect my thoughts and reorganize my energy, after which I felt so disappointed I trailed off home to my concrete pillar and stayed there for two days, suffering from acute depression.

Ghost friends told me I should have been more than pleased with myself. They pointed out, in their efforts to cheer me up, that in these days of disbelief in ghosts I should be proud of my success in scaring two mortals out of their wits. But I'm afraid I couldn't see it like that. I had made a hash of the thing I really wanted to do, and I had been professionally careless. There was no excuse for such things. And as a result I was paying the price: I was still slopping around in ghostly limbo. Not that it is a bad life, as lives go. But it is not the ultimate . . . not the life any sane soul desires. And when you are within range of that life, as I am now that I am dead, the desire becomes a yearning almost painfully strong. The wise old man who said that Hell is the yearning to be in Heaven was right after all. But I cannot satisfy that yearning until I can persuade some mortal that I *am* dead, that my earthly remains are safely stowed away among the steel girders and concrete pillars of the Sure Shield Insurance Building, Manchester.

Two days' rest worked wonders. I got over my depression, recharged myself, did a good deal of thinking. The third day I spent discussing my new ideas with the most experienced ghosts who lived within convenient range of my quarters in the pillar. The consensus of opinion was that I had two possible courses of action open to me. Neither was easy to pull off successfully.

I chose spirit possession first.

To get the best results from spirit possession, you need an emotionally unstable mortal with a vivid imagination and a mind open to suggestion. All the experts told me that teenage girls are admirable for the purpose. And I knew just the right one for me. My sister.

Angela is sixteen. She is emotionally so unstable that she is as happy as a lark one minute and weeping like a sick willow the next. Her imagination is vivid to the point of being lurid (at any rate, it allows her to see pimply teenage boys as Greek gods, which anyone has to admit takes a powerful imagination!). As for her mind, it is as pliant as warm putty. On the other hand, like most girls of her age, her constitution is as tough as tempered steel, so I had no fears of any ill effects on her health if my still rather amateur ghosting went badly wrong, as it had done with Harry. (Harry, by the way, recovered his car the next day in broad daylight, after which he had the local vicar exorcise it—something I regarded as extravagant cheek, seeing he never goes near a church from one year's end to the next.)

Angela would do nicely. She also had the added advantage of being one of the family; she would know who and what I was talking about without tiresome and lengthy explanations.

The only trouble was that possession takes a day or two to get going properly. Had I appreciated before I began how much hard work goes into it on the ghost's part, I'd certainly have dropped the entire idea at once. As it was, I went ahead with enthusiasm.

I gave the first night up to dream making. Well before Angela's normal bedtime, I settled myself in her room and began to compose myself for the task ahead, inventing the dreams I'd put into Angela's head once I'd got inside her—a tricky business in itself. When her bedtime came, I was fully in the spirit of the occasion.

Angela's bedtime came, but Angela did not. She did not even arrive home from an evening out until twelve thirty. By then my concentration was already a bit frayed; instead of feeling calm, collected, and spiritually prepared, I was irritable, out of joint, and sparking all over the place with nasty thoughts about my sister. I recalled ruefully that this was exactly the effect Angela had usually had on me during our earthly life together.

When at last she arrived home, Dad was waiting to haul her over the coals for being out so late without permission. They argued. Angela flounced up to her room. By this time she was in no condition for me or anyone else to possess her in any way at all. After slamming her door, she crashed around her room for a quarter of an hour giving vent to her temper; then for ten minutes she wept soulfully on her bed, just loudly enough for the parents to hear her but not so loud that either of them would come in and console her. Finally, she pulled off her clothes, threw them in a heap on the floor, and fell bad-tempered into bed, where she lay awake for ages inventing the most lurid and morbid fantasies I have yet encountered in anyone's mind, fantasies involving Dad, her boyfriend (who had kept her out late), and herself (in dramatic, romantic, and, needless to add, tragic situations).

I could hardly summon up enough brotherly affection and tenderness to go on with my plan. Indeed, for a while I was sorely tempted to give her the most bloodcurdling and spine-chilling haunt I could manage, just to teach her a lesson. But

Dead Trouble

eventually she drifted off to sleep, and I pulled myself together and went to work.

You'll appreciate that, at this point, I must leave out technical details. The method by which one gets inside another person to control their thoughts is difficult enough to explain to a spirit; it is almost impossible to do so to a mortal. But should a mortal by some chance understand the explanation, then they would possess information that would give them a power over others of an extraordinary kind. If this power fell into the wrong hands, you can see what evil could be let loose in the world.

All I can say is that for a couple of hours I gave Angela the treatment. I started out with pleasant memory dreams. I used one about the two of us years ago when she was still very small and I saved her from drowning in a seaside pool all of six inches deep. At least I told Mum I had saved her, and Angela was only too glad to take part in the deception because it sounded like such a dramatic story and she was the center of it. I used the one about the Christmas when she was thirteen and I gave her the first pair of nylons she had ever owned along with a gigantic box of Swiss chocolates (a rather spiteful gift actually, as she was trying to slim at the time, being just at the puppy-fat age). Then I brought back the time when I stood up for her against Mum and Dad; Angela wanted to stay out late at a party for the first time in her life. (This seemed an appropriate memory to recall, considering the events of the night!)

There was lots more of this kind of thing before I decided she had had enough. I juggled everything about, of course, and exaggerated bits here, suppressed unpleasant details there, and generally colored the dreams up so that everything was larger than life: A real potpourri of a dream, it was. By the time I was finished, Angela was in a very receptive mood indeed, whimpering with nostalgia for the happy times we'd had together. (In fact, we were always bickering and backbiting, but time and dreams, and death most of all, are powerful antidotes to people's recollections of the truth, as you'll have noticed, I expect.)

This done, I was ready to start on the big scene, a surrealist nightmare that Salvador Dalí would have been proud to invent. Angela saw me in every deadly situation imaginable. I fell from a cliff into swirling, angry waves over which the sun shone, but a sun that looked like a huge illuminated clock with the hands showing three thirty—the time at which I slipped into the mixer. I pictured her stirring a pan of porridge (she hates porridge!); she saw an insect threshing about in the pan, looked closer, saw it was not an insect but me! At that moment I disappeared under the surface and the oven clock rang its alarm bell with the hands pointing to three and six. On and on, until Angela was in a sweat of anxiety and was beginning to suspect what I wanted her to: that I was dead, and not just "missing." In the end she was moaning and shaking her head in her sleep, as if saying "No, no!"

All this took a vast amount of energy, and I was soon dangerously tired. I decided that, before things got out of control, I should get some rest and observe the outcome of my first night's work. But, just to make sure that Angela did not dismiss her dreams when she woke up, I waited until the morning light brought her back to consciousness. Then, as soon as she opened her eyes, I picked up a bottle of cold cream from her dressing table and hurled it across the room.

That did it. Angela was out of bed and into Mum's room without a second thought. There she poured out her confused dreams, confusing them all the more by trying to recount them to someone else. Mum thought Angela was ill; Dad as always listened calmly and said nothing. Angela insisted that her dreams were an omen, that I had not gone off somewhere secretly as everyone said, but that I had died somehow, and not very pleasantly. Mum burst into tears and told Angela not to talk like that. "Where there's life, there's hope," she said. Angela then burst into tears too, said no one ever had understood her but me, that she knew, just *knew,* her dreams meant that I was dead, and that she felt like running away and never coming back. Dad sighed deeply and got up, saying he felt like a nice cup of tea. After this,

Angela stormed from the room, dressed hurriedly, and left for school without eating any breakfast or saying another word.

I had the uneasy feeling that my attempt to get a message to my family via Angela was doomed to failure. But I pressed on.

The next night I repeated the dreams, but this time I ended them by engraving a mental picture of myself in a tragic pose deep in Angela's mind before throwing a few things around the room in best poltergeist fashion just as she woke up.

Once again Angela ran to Mum. She was so desperately convincing and distressed that Mum took her seriously, listening sympathetically to her story. Mum even came into Angela's room to see the mess I'd made. Dad went off at the first sign of trouble to make himself a cup of tea.

Angela, placated by Mum's sympathy and excited by the effect of her performance—she loves to be the central figure in a drama—set off for school in high spirits, and there recounted her tale to all and sundry, though only after swearing each person to secrecy and telling them it was all in the strictest confidence.

All that day I sat quietly smiling to myself; here was progress after all. Another night and I could reveal myself and the details of my death and departure.

The third night was much the same as the other two, with the addition of a ghostly and audible voice whispering "Angela ... Angela..." before my sister dropped off to sleep, and a bout of sleepwalking before I dispossessed her in the morning. I had every hope of complete success.

My hopes were soon dashed.

Angela woke pale, fatigued and dizzy. I had overdone things.

Mum took one look at the limp figure in the bed and sent for a doctor. There was, of course, nothing seriously the matter with the girl. True, she was tired and running a temperature. But all she needed was a day's rest.

The situation now got out of control. The doctor was suspicious, though he pretended otherwise to Angela. He prescribed a tranquilizer and told her to stay in bed. But downstairs, he told

Mum to "keep an eye on that girl and report any change in her condition." Mum was only too delighted to have an opportunity of mothering her only daughter and watched her every minute of the day and as much as she could manage of the following night.

Dad drank endless cups of tea.

Unimportant though these things may appear, they put me in a swivet. The tranquilizers made my task three times more difficult than before; my experience as a ghost was too limited to cope with the powers of modern medical science. Mum on the watch meant that if I tried a haunt she would be sure to see the effects, which would upset her more than I could bear. As for Dad's endless tea drinking: I recognized this as a sure sign that things were getting on top of him, and I had even less desire to upset him than I had to upset Mum. If he started worrying, the strain might affect his weak heart and for all I knew he'd end up joining me. This was a responsibility I dared not take.

For a day or two I let things ride, hoping Angela's health would improve, when I could start work again. But during the doctor's last visit, Mum had a long private chat with him, telling him all about Angela's dreams, and about the things being thrown around her room. The doctor said that he'd thought as much—he'd known at once that something was up. It was, he said, a common ailment among girls of Angela's age; the best thing would be to take Angela to a psychiatrist.

I dropped my plans like a hot brick then and there, and fled back to my pillar in the insurance building. Psychiatrists were the last people I wanted to tangle with—or to tangle with my sister; they can make haunting so complicated and mess one about so much that it just isn't worth the effort. (It doesn't surprise me one bit that this ghostly limbo-land is teeming with psychiatrists; more of them get stuck here than of any profession. And I've never heard of one of them getting through to the other side. Old Freud mopes around, muttering about sex, and Jung is always arguing with him and seeing archetypal patterns in the least likely places and events. They're a hopeless bunch!)

Dead Trouble

Well, my defeat at Mum's hands left me one more solution worth trying. Automatic writing. If this failed, then I was condemned to a desultory life in this ghostly state for years—maybe centuries—until someone accidentally found my remains in the insurance building. Luckily, modern buildings are made to last no more than a few years, so my prospects of being discovered were brighter than those of ghosts whose bodies are buried in ancient buildings that were built to last forever.

I consulted the experts once more. Having recovered their cool after the shock of hearing any ghost as inexperienced as myself announce that he was taking up automatic writing—something only the most advanced and knowledgeable haunters ever even contemplate—they gave me a lot of useful tips.

They warned me, for instance, not to employ professional mediums and clairvoyants. Professionals, they said, are usually phony anyway and have never made contact with anything more than their instinct for making money at the expense of the credulous. And those who are genuine spirit contacts, born with the power to speak the words spirit people put into their minds, are just like all actors: They love to add and take away from the original script. Never satisfied to let the spirit work through them, they can't resist adding a touch of detail there and missing the main point here, while they have an insatiable taste for melodrama: for dressing up in weird clothes, and rigging outlandish gimmicks, and upstaging any poor spirit who is foolish enough to get involved with them. No, my advisers said, they are an odd lot and best left alone.

"What you must do," they told me, "is find an ordinary person who is clairvoyant and doesn't know it. They are the people most likely to have the special makeup of personality you need to work through, while they won't try to take part themselves in writing your message."

I spent five weeks looking around for suitable mortals, ones with the right qualities for such difficult work as I had in mind: people pure in spirit, innocent in nature, neither naive nor over-wise. Above all they must possess great faith, faith in life as worth living despite its horrors and troubles, faith in human nature and the durability of that incomparably beautiful but elusive creation, the human soul. Such people, I discovered, are rare indeed.

But I found one in the end, though with a little thought I might have realized where to look and searched here first. I came to this old people's home on the edge of town only this evening. A deaf old man lives here, and has done so for the last twenty years since his wife died. He has two sons, both big men in business these days and very busy. Too busy ever to come and see the old man. He has a daughter too, but she has her own family to cope with and manages to visit only on special occasions like Christmas and her father's birthday.

So he passes his days alone, reading and thinking and watching the world go by in the silence of his being. For forty years he worked day in, day out, as a joiner. He loved his garden, brought his family up as tenderly as he cared for his tomatoes and sweet peas. From his early twenties the pride and joy of his life was his beloved wife, and she doted on him as much as he on her—though she sometimes pretended otherwise. Now she is gone, he is too old to garden, his children grown up and scattered. At first, after his wife's death, he grieved bitterly, but he conquered his grief, and every day that passes, his faith deepens in the world to come.

This is the man who now writes this message for me. My hope is that when he wakes and finds these hastily scribbled pages by his bedside, the pencil still clutched in his gnarled old hand, he will do me one further act of kindness, like the many others which have passed unnoticed in his life, and convey my news to my family. Or . . .

Perhaps not . . .

I begin to see that this old saint has something to teach me, who should be beyond teaching. . . .

Perhaps, old man, it is best that my sudden end and my curious whereabouts remain unknown. Perhaps I need time to dwell as much as you have done on the nature of life and death. Perhaps when I have done this and plumbed the depths of that knowledge, I will be ready to pass from this staging post of death into the life eternal—as ready as you are now to pass from mortality into immortality without a stopping place between.

Quite a thought!

Perhaps after all I am in this limbo-land for a purpose I had not understood. Till now.

I'm grateful to you, old man.

But I will leave this message by your side for your eyes only to see. It can be a sign to you that you have not lived in vain. After reading it, do with it as you please.

Peace . . .

NOTE: *These papers were by the bedside of Mr. James Henry Gibbons on the morning he was found dead, aged 78. I suppose they are the ramblings of a dying man's imagination.*

SIGNED, *A. C. Harris, Warden, The Hermitage*

The Shepherd's Dog

JOYCE MARSH

CHAUVAL LIFTED HIS HEAD SHARPLY; his sensitive, upstanding ears twitched as he listened intently. From outside the window a little twig scraped against the pane and the big white dog recognized it as the sound which had aroused him from his uneasy sleep. His body relaxed as he allowed his shaggy head to drop down onto his forepaws.

He did not sleep again, however, as his olive-green eyes, lightly flecked with little pinpoints of golden light, stared fixedly at the still form on the bed. For two long days he had watched that figure, waiting to see the tiniest movement of life, although by now his every sense told him that he hoped in vain.

On the first morning when the Master had not risen as he usually did at first light of day, Chauval had been impatient and slightly irritable. Even through the closed window his sensitive nose had picked up the exhilarating scent of the new day. His limbs had almost ached in their eagerness for that glorious, rushing scamper over the heather which began his every morning.

Restlessly he had padded around the room, scratched at the closed door and lifted his head to savor the fresh, clean smell of a new day. Then a long deep growl had begun low in his throat,

The Shepherd's Dog

but still the Master had not moved. The growl had become a whine, anxiety replaced impatience and Chauval had crept closer to the bed. He had thrust his nose beneath the Master's shoulder and nudged him violently. The man's head rolled on the pillow, but he had not opened his eyes nor made a sound. One still hand dangled from the bed; Chauval licked it—it was so cold.

Then the big, shaggy white dog had jumped onto the bed, covering the man with his body, licking at his face and hands as he tried to drive out that dreadful cold with the warmth of his own body.

It was then that the vague anxiety had become a sickening fear, for the Master's well-known scent had gone and in its place was a smell that Chauval knew and dreaded.

So many times in his long working life the sheepdog had found a sheep which had wandered too near the edge and had fallen to its death on the rocky beach below, or a straying lamb which had become stranded on a ledge to die of fear and hunger. All these animals had the smell of death on them, and now that same hateful scent was upon the Master.

Chauval, in his panic, had leaped from the bed and rushed first to the door and then to the window, his head lifted in a long, despairing wail. Instinctively he knew that with his great strength and size he could, if he chose, break out of the room, but without direct orders from the Master, he dared not try.

All his life, ever since he had first come as a tiny puppy to the lonely cliff-top cottage, the Master had ordered and directed his every action. It was the Master who had taught him how to guard sheep, it was he who had told the dog what to do and when to do it. Even in those carefree, happy moments when work was done and the shepherd's dog was at liberty to rush pell-mell over the springy turf and wind-scorched heather, Chauval never forgot the law of instant obedience, for his playtime began on the Master's command and ended with his whistling call.

Chauval had been happy and secure in his trusting devotion, but now the Master's voice was still and the dog was alone and desolate. In his bewilderment and confusion there was only one thing of which he could be certain. When he was alone, his duty was to stay on guard, so for two long days and nights he had been in his room. Even the gnawing hunger and thirst were forgotten as he crouched low, every muscle of his body tense and alert to protect his Master and his home.

Suddenly Chauval's head lifted again as another, much louder noise came from outside and the draft, blowing in through a broken pane, carried the scent of a human. Silently, but with his lip lifted in the beginnings of a snarl, Chauval moved to the window and raised himself on hind legs to look out.

On the path, a few yards from the cottage, stood a man. His head was thrown back as he shouted loudly:

"Are ye in there, Will? Are ye all right then, Will?"

Chauval looked back quickly toward the bed, half hoping that the sound of a voice might have called the Master back to life, but still there was no movement from the bed.

The dark-haired man, still calling the Master's name, had come very close to the cottage and was rapping on the door with his heavy stick. Chauval's snarl became more menacing and the hairs on his back stood up stiffly. He knew that man and he knew that stick. Once, a very long time ago, he had felt its weight upon his back; the man had come into the cottage while Chauval was alone and had walked into rooms and looked into places where only the Master was allowed to go. The dog had barked once in warning and the man had hit him with the stick. Now that man was an enemy—never to be allowed inside.

The knocking on the door had ceased as the man walked around the cottage, looking in at all the windows. He came to Chauval's window and stopped to peer inside. For a brief moment the man and the dog stared into each other's eyes. The sound of the dog's angry barking echoed in the room and the man leaped back in startled fear.

But he realized that he was protected by the glass between them and he came forward again to look past the frantic dog into the room. He stared in for a moment and then, turning quickly, he ran off. Chauval fell silent. In the distance he could hear the soft, melancholy bleating of the sheep and, further away still, the wild rushing of the sea hurling itself against the barren, rocky beach.

Stiffly he dropped down from the window and crept back to resume his vigil by the bed, but, weakened by lack of food and little sleep, the spate of barking had exhausted him and his eyes closed again in slumber.

A long time must have passed, for the room was almost dark when Chauval was once more aroused by the sound of footsteps and loud voices.

There was a violent banging on the cottage door and Chauval heard it fly open with a crash. Swiftly, he leaped onto the bed, crouching over the defenseless Master. He was sweating with fear and the perspiration ran off his tongue to hang in wet, sticky streams from his mouth.

The voices came nearer and nearer; the bedroom door flew open and in the opening was the Man with the Stick. The huge white dog remained motionless, hunched protectively and tense above his Master's body. His lip curled upward, showing long, yellow teeth, and the whites of his eyes gleamed through the dusk.

"The great ugly brute will ne'er let us come near. We'll have to shoot him first."

It was that harsh rough voice of the Man with the Stick. Chauval gathered himself to spring, but suddenly someone else spoke, softly and gently.

"Poor thing, he must have been locked in here for days. He's half-starved. Maybe I can coax him out."

The cruel voice muttered and mumbled, but the man stood aside and his place in the doorway was taken by a stranger.

"Good dog, come on then, we'll not hurt you; good boy, that's a good dog."

The stranger's voice was kind and reassuring. He held out the back of his hand with the fingers hanging limply down.

"Good dog, come here then."

With infinite slowness, Chauval eased himself off the bed. Never taking his eyes from the stranger's face, the dog crawled slowly across the floor. With all his heart he wanted to trust this man.

"For heaven's sake, get on with it. We haven't got all night to mess around with yon vicious brute."

The harsh voice spat out the words, and out of the corner of his eye Chauval saw the stick raised above him. With a powerful spring he leaped up, and his teeth fastened in the hand holding the stick. He felt the warm taste of blood in his mouth as his body thudded into the man's chest and bore him backward to the floor.

The room was full of noise and the smell of human fear. The stranger's voice, no longer gentle, was raised above the others and his was the hand which snatched up the stick and brought it down hard on the dog's back. With a yelp of pain and anger, Chauval turned to snarl in brief defiance at the stranger who was now another enemy and then he sprang past the men toward the open door. Frantic hands grabbed at his long fur but, snapping and snarling, the dog pulled himself free and leaped outside. With a few bounding strides he reached the cover of the bushes and threw himself down in the tangled bracken.

In an agony of confusion and fear, he stared at the cottage. He wanted to go back inside to continue his guard over the Master, but he dared not. Lights had sprung up in the windows and the sound of voices drifted out. The front door stood open and suddenly two men came out carrying something wrapped in white. Instinctively, Chauval knew that it was the Master.

The Man with the Stick had brought the strangers and Chauval had been driven out. They had forced him to abandon his post, and now his enemies were taking the Master away. The big dog raised himself up onto his haunches, his green eyes glittered in the twilight darkness and he began to whimper softly. Then he flung back his head, the long snout pointing directly upward toward the pale moon, and the whimper became a long howl of desolation and despair.

The Shepherd's Dog

"There he is, over there! Shoot him, someone, while ye've got the chance. He'll be no good now old Will's gone and if he turns rogue, he'll be a menace to all of us."

It was the harsh, cruel voice, and close upon the words came a sharp crack and a singing bullet passed close to the dog's ear.

Chauval began to run as he had never run in his life before. Leaping, bounding, with lolling tongue and eyes bulging until they were nearly bursting from the sockets, he crashed through the bracken and undergrowth.

The lights in the cottage receded to pinpoints and the shouts of the men were borne away on the night breeze, and still Chauval ran. The scrubby trees and bushes thinned and the ground beneath his feet became more sharp and rocky as he fled up the steep, craggy hill which rose sharply from the cliff-top pasture. At last he could run no more and he flung himself down onto a flat rock.

His sides heaved and the breath rasped in his throat. The pounding of his heart quieted at last and he breathed more easily, but now he was tormented by thirst.

The big dog raised his head and the sensitive nostrils quivered as he explored the night wind for the longed-for scent of water. His senses told him that water was not far away, but he did not immediately go to find it. Instead he peered anxiously down the slope and listened intently. In his headlong flight he had taken no care to hide his trail and his enemies could easily track him down.

To his relief he could hear only the sound of rushing wind; for the moment he was safe. Gleaming wraithlike in the darkness, the dog weaved a cautious zigzagging course toward the water. The clear mountain stream flowed abundantly. Bursting out from a fissure in the rock, it cascaded first into a deep pool before it ran off down the hillside. Chauval thrust his muzzle into the icy water and greedily drank his fill.

He was ravenously hungry, but the wild, rushing escape up the steep hill had drained the last of his strength and he was too exhausted to search for food. A flat, jutting shelf of rock offered him some shelter and he crept beneath it. Wearily he buried his nose into the long warm hairs on his flank and slept.

Chauval awoke at the first light of day and his first thought was the gnawing, agonizing hunger. He had never in his life needed to find his own food; no one had ever taught him how and now he had no idea where to begin. He whimpered and whined, calling for the Master. Even now he could still desperately hope to hear a whistle or the beloved voice calling his name, but all was silent except for the tinkling water and the lonely singing of the wind.

His green eyes flicked restlessly as he surveyed the barren hillside—there was no food here. There would be food in the cottage if only he dared go to find it. Hunger overcame fear at last and, moving carefully, with his body close to the ground, he crept down the hill.

The cottage was deserted: The strangers had gone and the Master had not returned. In the pale light of dawn, the dog moved around the house, scratching at the closed doors, but there was no way to get in. The sheep, left unguarded, had strayed into the tangled undergrowth near the cottage, where they bleated dismally. Instinctively Chauval moved around them, expertly gathering them into a little flock and herding them back to the grazing land. Enviously he watched them eat their fill of the succulent grass.

Suddenly he heard the sound of a single sheep in distress and behind a large rock he found a young ewe with her lamb stretched out on the ground beside her. It had fallen from the top of the rock and its fleece was streaked with blood. The mother bleated pathetically, but the lamb was quite dead. With an expert little rush, Chauval drove the ewe away and nudged the lamb with his nose. It was still warm and the sickly sweet smell of the fresh blood made the juices flow in his mouth, but it was forbidden to eat the flesh of a dead sheep and Chauval would not disobey the Master's law—he would die first.

"Good dog, you may eat the lamb."

The well-known voice sounded loud and clear in his ear. With

The Shepherd's Dog

a little yelp of joyful surprise, Chauval looked around. The breeze blew in off the sea and the sheep called softly to each other, but there was neither scent nor sight of the Master. Yet his voice came again, urgently.

"Eat, Chauval—eat or you will die."

The pangs of desperate hunger gnawed agonizingly at his insides, but there was no need now to hesitate. Somehow and from somewhere far off the Master had spoken.

The long yellow teeth ripped and tore at the soft flesh as, with ravenous haste, the dog wolfed down the fresh meat. So intent was he upon satisfying his hunger that he did not immediately notice that he was no longer alone on the cliff top. A man, a woman and a boy were running toward him. They were shouting and waving their arms when Chauval heard them at last and looked up from his meal. He gave a quick, welcoming bark, for he knew them and they were his friends. Suddenly the youth bent down and picked something up from the ground. The next moment a sharp, hard rock flew through the air to hit the dog a stinging blow on the head. He yelped in pain and surprise; there was no doubting now the menace in their voices and gestures. Suddenly and inexplicably even these friends had become his enemies. Once more he fled upward to safety. The full and satisfying meal had restored his strength and he moved swiftly.

The people stood by the bloody remnants of the lamb and watched him go.

"That was Will's old dog," the boy said.

"Aye and I should've had my gun handy. He'll have to be shot now—he's turned sheep killer."

The woman answered her husband and there was pity in her voice. "Poor thing. 'Twill be a mercy to put him down or like as not he'll starve to death, for he'll not let us near him, that's for sure."

And so the barren rocky hill became Chauval's home and refuge. Water he had in abundance, but food was a constant, nagging problem. Once or twice he had managed to catch a young rabbit, but mostly he lived by what he could scrounge or steal from the scattered cottages on the cliff top. He had always to take care to search for his food when the people were asleep, for at the very sight of him, they drove him off with sticks and stones and even guns.

At night or in the light of early dawn, he slunk down the hill, moving cautiously with his body close to the ground. The Master's voice had never come again to give him leave, so he would not touch the sheep. In the pale light he moved like a great white shadow through the flock, and they, knowing him to be their friend, never ceased their constant nibbling at the grass as he passed.

While the cottagers slept, he padded silently around their homes, sniffing and searching for the scraps they had thrown away. Sometimes he ate the foul-smelling mash which the good wives had put out for their chickens. At other times he found a clutch of eggs laid in the undergrowth by a straying hen. Once in his maraudings he was attacked by a little half-wild cat; he had killed it and in his desperation had eaten even that.

In the weeks since the Master had gone, the sheepdog had grown thin and gaunt. His long coat, wetted by the rain and dried by the sun and salt breezes, was filthy and matted. Twigs, thorns and brambles had become tangled in the long hairs, where they fretted and scratched his skin when he lay down.

At night, especially when the moon rode high in the heavens, he yearned so desperately for the Master that he lifted his snout to the stars and let forth a long, desolate howl. Below, in the little hamlet, the people would hear his mournful wail and shudder in their warm, cozy beds.

One morning he had been particularly unsuccessful in his search for food; the sun had risen and the cottagers were stirring, yet his ravenous hunger would not allow him to abandon his scavenging. Suddenly he heard a door opening nearby and, in a quick, panicky scamper, he made for a clump of bracken, where he pressed his body close to the ground and trembled.

The Shepherd's Dog

The cheerful sound of a woman's voice drifted out through the open door, and a few minutes later a tiny child, tottering on unsteady legs, came out into the garden. Chauval pressed down even further into the concealing bracken and his heart thudded painfully. The little boy was coming closer and the dog dared not move, for he could not escape without being seen.

With the casual curiosity of the very young, the child was peering into the bushes. Suddenly he saw the white dog and his eyes opened wide in surprise. For a moment he swayed uncertainly on chubby little legs and then plumped down in front of Chauval.

"Hello, doggy. Do you want thum buppy?" he lisped.

With trusting friendliness he offered a thick crust of bread liberally spread with butter. Chauval took the food gently in his front teeth and wolfed it down. The boy gurgled his pleasure and stretched out his little hand to scratch and tickle at the sensitive spot behind the dog's ears. It was so long since Chauval had felt a loving, friendly touch. His delight in it now made him forget even his hunger. He crept forward and rested his head on the child's lap.

"Does doggy want thum more buppy?"

The little boy scrambled clumsily to his feet.

"Come on, doggy, let's get more buppy."

He set off toward his home, encouraging his new friend to follow. Longing to feel again that loving, friendly touch, Chauval crawled out of his hiding place. With tail tucked between his legs and head hanging low, he slunk after the boy, but his progress was slow and the child grew impatient.

"Come on, silly doggy."

He grasped the dog's ears in both his little hands and tugged with all his strength. In an excess of grateful affection Chauval reached up and licked the baby's face, and it was at that moment that a piercing shriek rang out from the cottage doorway. A woman's voice shouted urgently:

"Husband, come quickly! The killer dog's got our Ian!"

Chauval leaped sideways and the child, startled by the note of fear in his' mother's voice, ran to hide himself in her skirts. The woman was thrust aside and her place in the doorway was taken by a man. It was the Man with the Stick, only now it was not a stick but a gun that he held in his hand.

The terrified dog raced for the concealing cover of the undergrowth, but he was too late. The shot sounded almost in his ear and the searing bullet ran along his side, gouging a deep, bloody welt in its path.

For a moment or two Chauval ran on and felt no pain, but after a while his limbs stiffened and every thudding step was agony to him. He knew he could never reach the safety of his rocky retreat and he veered off toward the only other hiding place he knew —the tall rock on the cliff, behind which he had found and eaten the lamb.

He reached the rock and crept gratefully into its concealing shadow, pressing himself as close as he could to the cool, rough rock.

The bullet wound was painful, and for a long while he diligently licked at it until his rough tongue had cleaned it and soothed the pain. Weakened by the lack of food, and exhausted by the effort, he fell into a deep sleep.

When he awoke, the sun had long since reached its peak and had begun on its slow slide down toward the sea. Chauval was thirsty, his nose felt hot and dry and the inside of his mouth burned feverishly. He longed for the cool waters of his mountain stream and he peered cautiously out of his hiding place. The sound of human voices drifted over to him and the dog drew back in alarm.

Not far away, across the rich green pasture, a man, a woman and several children were playing with a ball. They laughed and shouted in their play, but their gaiety brought neither comfort nor reassurance to Chauval. He knew that he had but to show himself and their happy voices would become rough and harsh as they came at him with their sticks and their guns.

The Shepherd's Dog

Behind him the sheer cliff dropped down to the sea. There was no escape that way and the only way to safety was barred by the group on the cliff top.

Patiently the big, white dog settled down to await his opportunity to slip past his enemies. As he watched, one of the children wandered away from the group and, unnoticed by the others, came toward Chauval and the cliff edge.

The breeze carried his scent to the dog's sensitive nose and he recognized the tiny boy who had befriended him that morning. The child tottered to the very edge and, with all the strength in his fat little arms, threw a pebble out over the cliff. He chuckled as it rattled and clattered onto the beach below.

So many times Chauval had seen the Master's sheep venture too near to the crumbling edge of the cliff, and he knew what should be done. Like the sheep, this human child should be herded back to safety. Yet, if he were to venture out, he would be seen and the man would attack.

The boy swayed dangerously on the very edge and Chauval could not decide what he must do. In his anxiety he whimpered softly.

As he watched the child with an ever-increasing confusion, there came upon him an icy chill and he began to tremble violently. A small misty cloud had drifted in from the sea, enveloping him in its clammy touch. The hairs on his neck bristled and then, from somewhere in the vapor which hung over him, came the voice he had so longed to hear.

"Chauval, my good Chauval," it called. "Go then, boy, fetch him back."

There was no hesitation now. The Master had spoken and Chauval leaped to obey.

"Steady boy, easy now," the voice called from behind, and the good sheepdog lay down in the grass. Then, quietly, so as not to startle the child, he moved forward in a series of little rushes. As soon as he was able, the dog placed himself between the boy and the cliff edge. The child, unafraid, lunged toward him, gurgling his pleasure, but with a warning snarl Chauval forced him back. Again the child came on, and this time the dog herded him away from the edge with a little nip on the fatty part of his leg. More startled than hurt, the boy gave a loud indignant wail and ran at his protector with his clenched fists—but again Chauval urged him backward from the cliffs.

The man and the woman had heard their son's cry and were hurrying to his rescue. Chauval paid them no heed as, with all the skill he had learned from guarding sheep, he forced the child to safety. It was the man who reached the child first and snatched him up in his arms.

"Get away, you evil brute."

He lashed out with his heavy boot. Chauval leaped back, but the blow caught him full in the chest, forcing him nearer to the edge. The man aimed yet another vicious kick and the dog felt his back legs slip away into space. The weight of his body dragged down and he clawed frantically at the soft turf with his front feet. For a brief moment he hung suspended, but his grip was too tenuous and he fell.

Tumbling and twisting, Chauval hurtled down. The seagulls flew up from their rocky perches and their shrieks mingled with the yowls of the doomed dog. His body smashed down onto the rocks and earth; sea and sky were blotted out in one final stab of pain.

The blood-streaked flanks heaved once, twice and were still. The birds settled back on the rocky ledges and, from above, the man and the woman looked down on the still shape so far below them.

"Well, that's the last trouble we'll get from that vicious dog," the man said with cruel satisfaction.

"Aye," said his wife, "an' it might have been our Ian lyin' doon there. We've only the dog to thank that it isn't."

The man looked askance.

"You're a fool, husband," she went on. "You've seen a dog work sheep often enough. Could ye not see that it weren't attack-

The Shepherd's Dog

ing our boy? He were herdin' him back from the edge—just like he would sheep."

The man hung his head. "Well, he's gone wild. He's better off this way, anyhow," he said sulkily.

"Aye," she said, and they moved off, while the child in his father's arms whined, "Nice doggy, where's 'at nice doggy gone?"

All was now very quiet upon the beach. The sun had dipped its rim into the sea and the shadows grew long and dark. A shrill whistle sounded in the breeze and a dark mist at the water's edge trembled like the heat haze of high summer. The misty cloud steadied and darkened and took shape. The whistle came again and a soft, white vapor hung over the body of the dead dog.

The cloud by the water's edge took on the shape of a man and he stretched forth his hand.

"Chauval."

The name was a soft sigh on the sea breeze. A great shaggy dog bounded forward, leaving behind the dead, bloodstained thing on the rocks.

The man moved off over the sands and the dog by his side leaped and danced in a transport of delight.

Few people now will venture down onto that part of the beach, for it is said that, in the late afternoon, just as the sun is about to slide into the sea, a man and his dog walk the sands. Those who have seen them say that the dog's olive-green eyes forever glow with a loving devotion, while the man smiles his contentment, and, as they pass, the air turns cold and is filled with soft sounds. Even the little waves breaking on the shore sing out the name . . . "Chauval, Chauval. . . ."

Meeting in the Park

RUTH RENDELL

STRANGE DISHEVELED WOMEN who had the air of witches sat around the table in Mrs. Cleasant's drawing room. One of them, a notable medium, seemed to be making some sort of divination with a pack of tarot cards. Later on, when it got dark, they would go on to table turning. The aim was to raise up the spirit of Mr. Cleasant, one year dead, and also, Peter thought with anger and disgust, to frighten Lisa out of her wits.

"Where are you going?" asked Mrs. Cleasant when Lisa came back with her coat on.

Peter answered for her. "I'm taking her for a walk in Holland Park, and then we'll have a meal somewhere."

"Holland Park?" said the medium. If a corpse could have spoken, it would have had a voice like hers. "Take care, be watchful. That place has a reputation."

The witch women looked at her expectantly, but the medium returned to her tarot and was eyeing the Empress, which she had brought within an inch or two of her long nose. Peter was sickened by the lot of them. Six months to go, he thought, and he'd take Lisa out of this—this coven.

It was a Sunday afternoon in spring, and the air in the park was fresh and clean, almost like country air. Peter drew in great gulps

Meeting in the Park

of it, cleansing himself of the atmosphere of that drawing room.

He wished Lisa would unwind, be less nervous and strung-up. The hand he wasn't holding kept going up to the charm she wore on a chain around her neck or straying out to knock on wood as they passed a fence.

Suddenly she said, "What did that woman mean about the park's reputation?"

"Some occult rubbish. How should I know? I hate that sort of thing."

"So do I," she said, "but I'm afraid of it."

"When we're married you'll never have to have any more to do with it. I'll see to that. God, I wish we could get married now or that you'd come and live with me till we can."

"I can't marry you till I'm eighteen without Mummy's permission, and if I live with you, they'll make me a ward of court."

"Surely not, Lisa."

"Anyway, there's only six months to wait. It's hard for me, too. Don't you think I'd rather live with you than with Mummy?"

The childish rejoinder made him smile. "Come on, try and look a bit more cheerful," he said. "I want to take your photograph. If I can't have you, I'll have your picture."

They had reached a sunny open space where he sat her on a log and told her to smile. He got the camera out of its case. "Don't look at those people, darling. Look at me."

It was a pity the man and the girl had chosen that moment to sit down on the wooden seat.

"Lisa!" he said sharply, and then he wished he hadn't, for her face crumpled with distress. He went up to her. "What's the matter, Lisa?"

"Look at that girl," she said.

"All right. What about her?"

"She's exactly like me. She's my double."

"Nonsense! What makes you say that? Her hair's the same color and you're about the same build, but apart from that there's no resemblance. She's years older than you and she's—"

"Peter, you must see it! She could be my twin. Look, the man with her has noticed. He looked at me and said something to her, and then they both looked."

Peter couldn't see more than a superficial similarity. "Well, supposing she were your double, which I don't for a moment admit, so what? Why get in such a state about it?"

"Don't you know about doubles? Don't you know that if you see your double, you're seeing your own death, that you will die within the year?"

"Oh, Lisa, come *on*! I never heard anything so foolish. This is more rubbish you've picked up from those crazy old witches. It's just sick superstition."

But nothing he could say calmed her. Her face had grown white and her eyes troubled. Worried for her rather than angry, he put out his hand and helped her to her feet. She leaned against him, trembling, and he saw she was clutching her amulet.

"Let's go," he said. "We'll find another place to take your picture. Don't look at her if it upsets you. Forget her."

When they had gone off along the path, the man on the seat said to his companion, "Couldn't you really see that girl was the image of you?"

"I've already told you, no."

"Of course you look a good deal older and harder, I'll give you that."

"Thank you."

"But you're almost her double. Take away a dozen years and a dozen love affairs, and you'd *be* her double."

"Stephen, if you're trying to start another row, just say so and I'll go home."

"I'm not starting anything. I'm fascinated by an extraordinary phenomenon. Holland Park's known to be a strange place. There's a legend you can see your own double here."

"I never heard that."

"Nevertheless, my dear Zoe, it is so. 'The Magus Zoroaster, my dead child, Met his own image walking in the garden.'"

[50]

Meeting in the Park

"Who said that?"

"Shelley. Superstition has it that if you see your own image you will die within the year."

She turned slowly to look at him. "Do you want me to die within the year, Stephen?"

He laughed. "Oh, you won't die. You didn't see her, *she* saw you. And it frightened her. He was taking her photograph, did you see? I wish I'd asked him to take one of you two together. Why don't we see if we can catch up with them?"

"You know, you have a sick imagination."

"No, only a healthy curiosity. Come along now, if we walk fast we'll catch them at the gate."

"If it amuses you," said Zoe.

Peter and Lisa didn't see the other couple approaching. They were walking with their arms around each other, and Peter had managed to distract her from the subject of her double by talking of their wedding plans. At the northern gate someone behind him called out, "Excuse me!" and he turned to see the man who had been sitting on the seat.

"Yes?" Peter said rather stiffly.

"I expect you'll think this is frightful cheek, but I saw you back there and I was absolutely—well, struck by the likeness between my girlfriend and the young lady with you. There is a terrific likeness, isn't there?"

"I don't see it," said Peter, not daring to look at Lisa. (What a beastly thing to happen! He felt dismay.) "Frankly, I don't see any resemblance at all."

"Oh, but you *must*. Look, what I want is for you to do me an enormous favor and take a picture of them together. Will you? Do say you will."

Peter was about to refuse, and not politely, when Lisa said, "Why not? Of course he will. It's such a funny coincidence, we ought to have a record of it."

"Good girl! We'd better introduce ourselves then, hadn't we? I'm Stephen Davidson and this is Zoe Conti."

"Lisa Cleasant and Peter Milton," said Peter, still half stunned by Lisa's warm response.

"Hello, Lisa and Peter. Lovely to know you. Now, you two girls go and stand over there in that spot of sunshine."

So Peter took the photograph and said he'd send Stephen and Zoe a print when the film was developed. She gave him the address of the flat she and Stephen shared, and he noted it was but two streets over from his. They might have walked there together, which was what Stephen, remarking on this second coincidence, seemed to want. But seeing the tense, strained look in Lisa's eyes, Peter refused, and they separated on Holland Park Avenue.

"You didn't mind about not going with them, did you?" said Lisa.

"Of course not. I'd rather be alone with you."

"I'm glad," she said, and then, "I did it for you."

He understood. She had done it for him, to prove to him she could conquer her superstitious terrors. For his sake, because he wanted it, she would try. He took her in his arms and kissed her.

She leaned against him. He could feel her heart beating. "I won't tell anyone else about it," she said, and he knew she meant her mother and the witch women.

When the film was developed he didn't show it to her. He would send Zoe and Stephen their print and that would end the whole incident. But when he was putting it into an envelope, he realized he would have to write a covering note, which was a bore, as he didn't like writing letters. Besides, if he was going to take it to the post office, he might as well take it to their home. And one evening he did.

He had no intention of going in. But as he was slipping the envelope into the letter box, Zoe appeared behind him on the steps.

"Come in and have a drink."

He couldn't think of an excuse, so he accepted. She led him up two flights of stairs, looking at the photograph as she went.

"So much for this supposed fantastic likeness," she said. "Could you ever see it?"

Peter said he couldn't, wondering how Lisa could have been so silly as to fancy she had seen her double in this woman of thirty, who tonight had a drawn and haggard look. "It was mostly in your friend's imagination," he said as they entered the flat. "We'll see what he says about it now."

For a moment she didn't answer. When her reply came, it was brusque. "He's left me."

Peter was embarrassed. "I'm sorry." He looked into her face, at the eyes whose dark sockets were like bruises. "Are you very unhappy?"

"I won't take an overdose, if that's what you mean. We'd been together for four years. It's hard to take. But I won't bore you with it. Let's talk about something else."

Peter had only meant to stay a few minutes, but the minutes grew into an hour, and when Zoe said she was going to cook dinner and would he stay and have it with her, he agreed.

She was interesting to talk to. She was a music therapist, and she talked about her work and played records. When they had finished their meal, a simple but excellent one, she reverted to her own private life and told him something of her relationship with Stephen. But she spoke without self-pity. And she could listen as well as talk.

It meant something to him to be able to confide in a mature, well-balanced woman who heard him out without interruption while he spoke of himself and Lisa—how they were going to be married when she was eighteen and when she would inherit half of her dead father's fortune. Not, he said, that the money had really anything to do with it. He'd have preferred her to be penniless. All he wanted was to get her away from that unhealthy atmosphere of dabbling with the occult, from that cloistral home where she was sheltered yet corrupted.

"What is she afraid of?" asked Zoe when he told her about the wood touching and the indispensable amulet.

He shrugged. "Of fate? Of some avenging fury that will resent her happiness?"

"Or of loss," said Zoe. "She lost her father. Perhaps she's afraid of losing you."

"That's the last thing she need be afraid of," he said.

It was midnight before he left. The next day he meant to tell Lisa where he had been. There were no secrets between them. But Lisa was nervous and uneasy—she and Mrs. Cleasant had been to a spiritualist meeting—and he thought it unwise to raise once more a subject that was better forgotten. So he said nothing. After all, he would never see Zoe again.

But a month or so later, a month in which he and Lisa had been happy and tranquil together, he met the older girl by chance in the Portobello Road. While they talked, it occurred to him that he had eaten a meal in her flat and that he owed her dinner. He and Lisa would take her out to dinner.

In her present mood Lisa would like that, and it would be good for her to see, after the lapse of time, how her superstitiousness had led her into error. He put the invitation to Zoe, who hesitated, then accepted when he explained it would be a threesome. Dinner, then, in a fortnight's time and he and Lisa would call for her.

"I met that girl Zoe and asked her to have dinner with us. All right with you?"

The frightened-child look came back into Lisa's face.

"Oh, no, Peter! I thought you understood. I don't ever want to see her again."

"But why not? You've seen the photograph, you've seen how silly those ideas of yours were. And Stephen won't be there. I know you didn't like him and neither did I. But they're not together anymore. He's left her."

She shivered. "Let's not get to know her, Peter."

"I've invited her," he said. "I can't go back on that now."

When the evening came, Zoe appeared at her door in a long

Meeting in the Park

gown, her hair dressed on top of her head. She looked majestic, mysteriously changed.

"Where's Lisa?" she asked.

"She couldn't come. She and her mother are going on holiday to Greece tomorrow and she's busy packing."

Part of this was true. He said it confidently, as if it were wholly true. He couldn't take his eyes off the new, transformed Zoe, and he was glad he had reserved a table in an exclusive restaurant.

In the soft lamplight her youth came back to her. And for the first time he was aware of the likeness between her and Lisa. The older and the younger sister, by a trickery of light and cosmetics and maybe of his own wistful imagination, had come together in years and become twins.

It might have been his Lisa who spoke to him across the table, across the silver and glass and the single rose in a vase, but a Lisa whom life and experience had matured. Never could Lisa have talked like this—of books and music and travel—or listened to him so responsively or advised with such wisdom. He was sorry when the evening came to an end and he left her at her door.

Lisa seemed to have forgotten his engagement to dine with Zoe. She didn't mention it, so he didn't either. On the following morning she was to leave with her mother for the month's holiday the doctor had recommended for Mrs. Cleasant's health.

"I wish I wasn't going," she said to Peter. "You don't know how much I'll miss you."

"Won't I miss *you*?"

"Take care of yourself. I'll worry in case anything happens to you. You mustn't laugh, but when my father was alive and went away from us, I used to listen to the news four or five times a day in case there was a plane crash or a train wreck."

"You're the one that's going away, Lisa."

"It comes to the same thing." She put up her hand to the charm she wore. "I've got this, but you—would you take my four-leaf clover if I gave it to you?"

"I thought you'd given up all that nonsense," he said, and his

[55]

disappointment in her almost spoiled their farewells. She kissed him good-bye with a kind of passionate sadness.

"Write to me," she said. "I'll write to you every day."

Her letters started coming at the end of the first week. They were the first he had ever had from her and they were like school essays written by a geography student, with love messages for the class teacher inserted here and there. They left him unsatisfied, a little peevish. He was lonely without her, but afraid of the image of her he carried with him.

He needed to talk it over and after a few days of indecision he telephoned Zoe. Ten minutes later he was in her flat, drinking her coffee and listening to her music. To be with her was a greater comfort than he had thought possible, for in the turn of her head, in the certain way she had of smiling, in the way her hair grew from a widow's peak on her forehead, he caught glimpses of Lisa.

And yet on that occasion he said nothing of his fears but, "I can't understand why I thought you and Lisa weren't alike."

"I didn't see it."

"It's almost overpowering. It's uncanny."

She smiled. "If it helps you to come and see me to get through the time while she's away, that's all right with me, Peter. I can understand that I remind you of her and that it makes things easier for you."

"It isn't only that," he said. "You mustn't think it's only that."

She said no more. It wasn't her way to probe, to hold inquisitions, or to set an egotistical value on herself. But the next time they were together he explained without being asked, and his explanation was appalling to him, the words more powerful and revealing than the thoughts from which they had sprung.

"It isn't true you remind me of Lisa. That's not it. It's that I see in you what she *might* become, only she never will."

"Who would want to be like me?"

"Everyone. Every young girl. Because you're what a woman should be, Zoe, clever and sane and kind and self-reliant and— beautiful."

"And if that's true," she said lightly, "though I disagree, why shouldn't Lisa become like that?"

"Because when she's eighteen, she'll be rich, an heiress. She'll never have to work for her living or have to struggle or learn. We'll live in a house near her mother and she'll get more and more like her mother, vain and neurotic, living on sleeping pills, spending all her time with spiritualists and getting involved in sick cults. When I look at you I don't see Lisa's double. I see *her*, an alternative she, if you like, twelve years ahead in time if another path had been marked out for her life. And at the same time I see you as you'd be if you'd led the sort of life she must and will lead."

"You can help her not to lead that life if you love her," said Zoe.

And then Lisa's letters stopped coming. A week went by without a letter. He had resolved, because of what was happening to him, not to see Zoe again. But she lived so near and he thought of her so often that he was unable to resist.

He went to her and told a lie that he had convinced himself was the truth. Lisa was too young to have a firm and faithful love for anyone. Her letters had grown cold and finally had ceased to come.

Zoe listened to him, to his urgent persuasion, his comparison of his forsaken state with her own, and when he kissed her, she responded at first with doubt, then with an ardor born of her own loneliness. They made love. When, later, he asked her if he might stay the night, she said he could.

After that he spent every night with her. He hardly went home. When he did, he found ten letters waiting for him at the doormat. Lisa and her mother had gone on to some Aegean island—the home of a mystic Mrs. Cleasant longed to meet—where the mail was uncertain. He read the childish letters, the "darling Peter, I miss you, I'll never go away again," with impatience and guilt—and then he went back to Zoe.

Why did he have to mention those letters to her? He wished

[57]

he hadn't. It was for her wisdom and her honesty that he had wanted her, and now those very qualities were striking back at him.

"When is she coming home?"

"Next Saturday," he said.

"Peter, I don't know what you mean to do—leave me and marry her or leave her and stay with me. And you must tell her about us, whatever you decide."

"I can't do that!"

"You must. Either way, you must. And if you mean to stay with me, what alternative have you?"

Stay with them both until he was sure, until he knew for certain. "You know I can't be without you, Zoe. But I can't tell her, not yet. She's such a child."

"You're going to marry that child. You love her."

"Do I?" he said. "I thought I did."

"I won't be a party to deceiving her, Peter. You must understand that. If you won't promise to tell her, I can't see you again."

Perhaps when he saw Lisa . . .

He went across the park to her mother's house on the Sunday evening. The medium was there and another woman who looked like a participant in a Black Mass, earnestly listening to Mrs. Cleasant's account of the mystic on the Aegean island and his investigations into the mysteries of the Great Pyramid. Lisa rushed into his arms, actually crying with happiness.

"This child has dreamed about you every night, Peter," said Mrs. Cleasant with one of her weird faraway looks. "Such dreams she has had! Of course she's psychic like me. When we knew the posts were delayed, I wanted her to get a message through to you by the Power of Thought, but she was unwilling."

"I knew you wouldn't like it," said Lisa. She stayed in his arms. Of course he couldn't tell her. In time, maybe, if he got their wedding postponed and let things cool down and—but it was out of the question to tell her now.

Meeting in the Park

He told Zoe he had. In order to see her again he had to do that.

"How did she take it?"

"Oh, quite well," he lied. "A lot of men have been paying her attention on holiday. I think she's beginning to realize I'm not the only man in the world."

"And she accepts—us?"

Why did she have to persist? Why make it so painful for him? He spoke boldly but with an inner self-disgust.

"I daresay she sees it as a key to her own freedom."

Zoe was convinced. The habitual truth-teller is reluctant to suspect falsehood in others. "Of course I've only met her once, and then only for a few minutes. But I wonder if you weren't deceiving yourself, Peter, when you said she loved you so much. You aren't going to see her again?"

He said he wasn't. He said it was all over, they had parted. But the enormity of what he had done appalled him. And when next he was with Lisa he found himself telling her all over again, and meaning it, how much he loved her and longed to take her away. Was he going to sacrifice that childish passionate love for a woman five years older than himself? The two were, in so many ways, alike. Suppose, in time to come, he grew tired of the one and regretted the other?

Yet, that night, he went back to Zoe.

With a skillful but frightening intrigue, he divided his time between the two of them. It wasn't too difficult. Social—and occult—demands were always being made on Lisa. Zoe believed him when he said he had been kept late at work.

Autumn came, and it was still going on, this double life. His need for, his dependence on Zoe intensified and he had begun to resent every moment he spent away from her. But Lisa and her mother had fixed the wedding date and with fatality he accepted its inexorable approach.

On an afternoon in October he was to meet Zoe in Holland

Park, by the northern gate. Lisa was going for a fitting of her wedding dress and afterward she was to dine with her mother in what he called the medium's lair. So that was all right. He waited by the gate for nearly an hour.

When Zoe didn't come, he went to her flat but received no answer to his ring. From his own home he telephoned her five times during the evening, but each time the bell rang in emptiness. He passed a sleepless night, the first night he had been on his own for four months.

All the next day, from work, he kept trying to call her, and for the first time since he had known her he made no call to Lisa. But his own phone was ringing when he got home at six. Of course it was Zoe, it must be. He took up the receiver and heard the frightened voice of Mrs. Cleasant.

"Peter?"

Disappointment hurt him like pain. "Yes," he said. "How are you? How's Lisa?"

"Peter, I have very bad news. I think you had better come here. Yes, now. At once."

"What is it? Has anything happened to Lisa?"

"Lisa has—passed over. Last night she took an overdose of my pills. I found her dead this morning."

He went out again at once. In the park, at dusk, the leaves were dying, some already fallen. At this spot, when the leaves had been showing their first green of spring, he had taken the photograph; at this spot he had seated her in a sunny open space and she had first seen Zoe.

Mrs. Cleasant wasn't alone. Some of the members of her magic circle were with her, but she was calmer than he had ever seen her and he guessed she was drugged.

"How did it happen?" he said.

"I told you. She took an overdose."

"But—why?" He shrank away from the medium's eyes which, staring, seemed to see ghosts behind him.

"Nothing to do with you, Peter," said Mrs. Cleasant. "She

loved you, you know that. And she was so happy yesterday. Her fitting was canceled. She said she wanted some fresh air because it was such a lovely day, and then she'd walk over to see you. She'd thrown away her charm—that amulet she wore—because she said you didn't like it. I told her not to—it was a harmless thing and might do good. Who knows? If she had been wearing it—"

"Ah, if she had been under the Protection!" said the medium.

Mrs. Cleasant went on, "We were going out to dinner. I waited and waited for her. When she didn't come I went out alone. I thought she was with you, safe with you. But I came back early and there she was, looking so tired and afraid. She said she was going to bed. I asked her if there was anything wrong and she said—"

Mrs. Cleasant's voice quavered into sobs and the witch women fluttered about her, touching her and murmuring.

It was the medium who explained in her corpse voice. "She said she had seen her own double in the park."

"But that was six months ago," he burst out. "That was in April!"

"No, she saw her own double yesterday afternoon, her image walking in the park. And she dared to speak to it. She told me her double spoke of love and of her lover."

He ran away from them then, out of the house. He hailed a taxi and in a shaking whisper asked the driver to take him to where Zoe lived. All the lights were on in her windows. He rang the bell, rang it again and again.

Then, while the lights still blazed but she didn't come down, he hammered on the door with his fists, calling her name. When he knew she wasn't going to come down, that he had lost her, her double and her, he sank down on the doorstep and wept.

The taxi driver, returning along the street in search of a fare, supposed him to be drunk, and learning his address from the broken mutterings, took him home.

He never saw Zoe again.

The Cyprian Cat

DOROTHY SAYERS

IT'S EXTRAORDINARILY DECENT OF YOU to come along and see me like this, Harringay. Believe me, I do appreciate it. It isn't every busy attorney who'd do as much for such a hopeless sort of client. I only wish I could spin you a more workable kind of story, but honestly, I can only tell you exactly what I told Peabody. Of course, I can see he doesn't believe a word of it, and I don't blame him. He thinks I ought to be able to make up a more plausible tale than that—and I suppose I could, but what's the use? One's almost bound to fall down somewhere if one tries to swear to a lie. What I'm going to tell you is the absolute truth. I fired one shot and one shot only, and that was at the cat. It's funny that one should be hanged for shooting at a cat.

Merridew and I were always the best of friends, school and college and all that sort of thing. We didn't see very much of each other after the war, because we were living at opposite ends of the country, but we met in town from time to time and wrote occasionally, and each of us knew that the other was there in the background, so to speak. Two years ago, he wrote and told me he was getting married. He had just turned forty and the girl was fifteen years younger, and he was tremendously in love. It gave me a bit of a jolt—you know how it is when your friends marry. You feel they will never be quite the same again, and I'd got used to the idea that Merridew and I were cut out to be old bachelors. But of course I congratulated him and sent him a wedding present, and I did sincerely hope he'd be happy. He was obviously head over heels; almost dangerously so, I thought, considering all things. Though except for the difference in age, it seemed suitable enough. He told me he had met her at—of all places—a rectory garden party down in Norfolk, and that she had actually never been out of her native village. I mean, literally—not so much as a trip to the nearest town. I'm not trying to convey that she wasn't first-class, or anything like that. Her father was some queer sort of recluse—a medievalist, or something—desperately poor. He died shortly after their marriage.

I didn't see anything of them for the first year or so. Merridew is a civil engineer, you know, and he took his wife away after the honeymoon to Liverpool, where he was doing something in connection with the harbor. It must have been a big change for her from the wilds of Norfolk. I was in Birmingham, with my nose kept pretty close to the grindstone, so we only exchanged occasional letters. His were what I can only call deliriously happy, especially at first. Later on, he seemed a little worried about his wife's health. She was restless; town life didn't suit her; he'd be glad when he could finish up his Liverpool job and get her away into the country. There wasn't any doubt about their happiness, you understand—she'd got him body and soul as they say, and as far as I could make out, it was mutual. I want to make that perfectly clear.

Well, to cut a long story short, Merridew wrote to me at the beginning of last month and said he was just off to a new job—a waterworks extension scheme down in Somerset, and he asked if I could possibly cut loose and join them there for a few weeks. He wanted to spend time with me, and Felice was longing to make my acquaintance. They had got rooms at the village inn. It was rather a remote spot, but there was fishing and scenery and so forth, and I should be able to keep Felice company while he was working up at the dam. I was about fed up with Birmingham, what with the heat and one thing and another, and it looked pretty good to me, and I was due for a holiday anyhow, so I fixed up to go. I had a bit of business to do in town, which I calculated would take me about a week, so I said I'd go down to Little Hexham on June 20th.

As it happened, my business in London finished itself off unexpectedly soon, and on the sixteenth I found myself absolutely free and stuck in a hotel with road drills working just under the windows and a tar-spraying machine to make things livelier. You remember what a hot month it was—flaming June and no mistake about it. I didn't see any point in waiting, so I sent off a wire to Merridew, packed my bag and took the train for Somerset the same evening. I couldn't get a compartment to myself, but I found a first-class smoker with only three seats occupied, and stowed myself thankfully into the fourth corner. There was a military-looking old boy, an elderly female with a lot of bags and baskets, and a girl. I thought I should have a nice, peaceful journey.

So I should have, if it hadn't been for the unfortunate way I'm built. It was quite all right at first—as a matter of fact, I think I was half-asleep, and I only woke up properly at seven o'clock, when the waiter came to say that dinner was on. The other people weren't taking it, and when I came back from the restaurant car I found that the old boy had gone, and there were only the two women left. I settled down in my corner again, and gradually, as we went along, I found a horrible feeling creeping over me that there was a cat in the compartment somewhere. I'm one of those wretched people who can't stand cats. I don't mean just that I prefer dogs—I mean that the presence of a cat in the same room with me makes me feel like nothing on earth. I can't describe it, but I believe quite a lot of people are affected that way. Something to do with electricity, or so they tell me. I've read that very often the dislike is mutual, but it isn't so with me.

The Cyprian Cat

The brutes seem to find me abominably fascinating—make a beeline for my legs every time. It's a funny sort of complaint, and it doesn't make me at all popular with dear old ladies.

Anyway, I began to feel more and more awful, and I realized that the old girl at the other end of the seat must have a cat in one of her innumerable baskets. I thought of asking her to put it out in the corridor, or calling the guard and having it removed, but I knew how silly it would sound and made up my mind to try and stick it. I couldn't say the animal was misbehaving itself or anything, and she looked a pleasant old lady; it wasn't her fault that I was a freak. I tried to distract my mind by looking at the girl.

She was worth looking at, too—very slim and dark-haired, with one of those dead-white skins that make you think of magnolia blossoms. She had the most astonishing eyes, too—I've never seen eyes quite like them: a very pale brown, almost amber, set wide apart and a little slanting, and they seemed to have a kind of luminosity of their own, if you get what I mean. I don't know if this sounds—I don't want you to think I was bowled over, or anything. As a matter of fact she held no sort of attraction for me, though I could imagine a different type of man going crazy over her. She was just unusual, that was all. But however much I tried to think of other things, I couldn't get rid of the uncomfortable feeling, and eventually I gave it up and went out into the corridor. I just mention this because it will help you to understand the rest of the story. If you can only realize how perfectly awful I feel when there's a cat about—even when it's shut up in a basket—you'll understand better how I came to buy the revolver.

Well, we got to Hexham Junction, which was the nearest station to Little Hexham, and there was old Merridew waiting on the platform. The girl was getting out too—but not the old lady with the cat, thank goodness—and I was just handing her luggage out after her when he came galloping up and hailed us.

"Hullo!" he said. "Why that's splendid! Have you introduced

yourselves?" So I tumbled to it then that the girl was Mrs. Merridew, who'd been up to town on a shopping expedition, and I explained to her about my change of plans and she said how jolly it was that I could come—the usual things. I noticed what an attractive low voice she had and how graceful her movements were, and I understood—though, mind you, I didn't share—Merridew's infatuation.

We got into his car—Mrs. Merridew sat in the back and I got up beside Merridew, and was very glad to feel the air and to get rid of the oppressive electric feeling I'd had in the train. He told me the place suited them wonderfully and had given Felice an absolutely new lease on life, so to speak. He said he was very fit, too, but I thought myself that he looked rather fagged and nervy.

You'd have liked that inn, Harringay. The real, old-fashioned stuff, as quaint as you make 'em, and everything genuine—none of your Tottenham Court Road antiques. We'd all had our grub, and Mrs. Merridew said she was tired; so she went up to bed early, and Merridew and I had a drink and went for a stroll round the village. It's a tiny hamlet quite at the other end of nowhere; lights out at ten, little thatched houses with pinched-up attic windows like furry ears—the place purred in its sleep. Merridew's working gang didn't sleep there, of course—they'd run up huts for them at the dams, a mile beyond the village.

The landlord was just locking up the bar when we came in—a block of a man with an absolutely expressionless face. His wife was a thin, sandy-haired woman who looked as though she was too downtrodden to open her mouth. But I found out afterward that was a mistake, for one evening when he'd taken one or two too many and showed signs of wanting to make a night of it, his wife sent him off upstairs with a gesture and a look that took the heart out of him. That first night she was sitting in the porch and hardly glanced at us as we passed her. I always thought her an uncomfortable kind of woman, but she certainly kept her house most exquisitely neat and clean.

They'd given me a noble bedroom, close under the eaves with

The Cyprian Cat

a long, low casement window overlooking the garden. The sheets smelled of lavender, and I was between them and asleep almost before you could count to ten. I was tired, you see. But later in the night I woke up. I was too hot, so took off some of the blankets and then strolled across to the window to get a breath of air. The garden was bathed in moonshine, and on the lawn I could see something twisting and turning oddly. I stared a bit before I made it out to be two cats. They didn't worry me at that distance, and I watched them for a bit before I turned in again. They were rolling over one another and jumping away again and chasing their own shadows on the grass, intent on their own mysterious business—taking themselves seriously, the way cats always do. It looked like a kind of ritual dance. Then something seemed to startle them, and they scampered away.

I went back to bed, but I couldn't get to sleep again. My nerves seemed to be all on edge. I lay watching the window and listening to a kind of soft rustling noise that seemed to be going on in the big wisteria that ran along my side of the house. And then something landed with a soft thud on the sill—a great Cyprian cat.

What did you say? Well, one of those striped gray and black cats. Tabby, that's right. In my part of the country they call them Cyprus cats, or Cyprian cats. I'd never seen such a monster. It stood with its head cocked sideways, staring into the room and rubbing its ears very softly against the upright bar of the casement.

Of course, I couldn't do with that. I shooed the brute away, and it made off without a sound. Heat or no heat, I shut and fastened the window. Far out in the shrubbery I thought I heard a faint meowing, then silence. After that, I went straight off to sleep again and lay like a log till the girl came in to call me.

The next day, Merridew ran us up in his car to see the place where they were making the dam, and that was the first time I realized that Felice's nerviness had not been altogether cured. He showed us where they had diverted part of the river into a swift little stream that was to be used for working the dynamo of an electrical plant. There were a couple of planks laid across the stream, and he wanted to take us over to show us the engine. It wasn't extraordinarily wide or dangerous, but Mrs. Merridew peremptorily refused to cross it and got quite hysterical when he tried to insist. Eventually he and I went over and inspected the machinery by ourselves. When we got back, she had recovered her temper and apologized for being so silly. Merridew abased himself, of course, and I began to feel a little *de trop.* She told me afterward that she had once fallen into a river as a child and nearly drowned, and it had left her with a—what d'you call it—a complex about running water. And but for this one trifling episode, I never heard a single sharp word pass between them all the time I was there, nor, for a whole week, did I notice anything else to suggest a flaw in Mrs. Merridew's radiant health. Indeed, as the days wore on to midsummer and the heat grew more intense, her whole body seemed to glow with vitality. It was as though she were lit up from within.

Merridew was out all day and working very hard. I thought he was overdoing it and asked him if he was sleeping badly. He told me that, on the contrary, he fell asleep every night the moment his head touched the pillow, and—what was most unusual with him—had not dreams of any kind. I myself felt well enough, but the hot weather made me languid and disinclined for exertion. Mrs. Merridew took me out for long drives in the car. I would sit for hours, lulled into a half slumber by the rush of warm air and the purring of the engine, and gazing at my driver, upright at the wheel, her eyes fixed unwaveringly upon the spinning road. We explored the whole of the country to the south and east of Little Hexham, and once or twice went as far north as Bath. Once I suggested that we should turn eastward over the bridge and run down into what looked like rather beautiful wooded country, but Mrs. Merridew didn't care for the idea; she said it was a bad road and that the scenery on that side was disappointing.

The Cyprian Cat

Altogether, I spent a pleasant week at Little Hexham, and if it had not been for the cats, I should have been perfectly comfortable. Every night the garden seemed to be haunted by them—the Cyprian cat that I had seen the first night of my stay, and a little ginger one and a horrible stinking black tom were especially tiresome, and one night there was a terrified white kitten that meowed for an hour on end under my window. I flung boots and books at my visitors till I was heartily weary, but they seemed determined to make the inn garden their rendezvous. The nuisance grew worse from night to night; on one occasion I counted fifteen of them, sitting on their hind ends in a circle, while the Cyprian cat danced her shadow dance among them, working in and out like a weaver's shuttle. I had to keep my window shut, for the Cyprian cat evidently made a habit of climbing up by the wisteria. The door, too; for once when I had gone down to fetch something from the sitting room, I found her on my bed, kneading the coverlet with her paws—*pr'rp, pr'rp, pr'rp*—with her eyes closed in a sensuous ecstasy. I beat her off, and she spat at me as she fled into the dark passage.

I asked the landlady about her, but she replied rather curtly that they kept no cat at the inn, and it is true that I never saw any of the beasts in the daytime, but one evening about dusk I caught the landlord in one of the outbuildings. He had the ginger cat on his shoulder and was feeding her with something that looked like strips of liver. I remonstrated with him for encouraging the cats about the place and asked whether I could have a different room, explaining that the nightly caterwauling disturbed me. He half opened his slits of eyes and murmured that he would ask his wife about it, but nothing was done, and in fact I believe there was no other bedroom in the house.

And all this time the weather got hotter and heavier, working up for thunder, with the sky like brass and the earth like iron, and the air quivering over it so that it hurt your eyes to look at it.

All right, Harringay—I am trying to keep to the point. And

I'm not concealing anything from you. I say that my relations with Mrs. Merridew were perfectly ordinary. Of course I saw a good deal of her because, as I explained, Merridew was out all day. We went up to the dam with him in the morning and brought the car back, and naturally we had to amuse one another as best we could till the evening. She seemed quite pleased to be in my company, and I couldn't dislike her. I can't tell you what we talked about—nothing in particular. She was not a talkative woman. She would sit or lie for hours in the sunshine, hardly speaking—only stretching out her body to the light and heat. Sometimes she would spend a whole afternoon playing with a twig or pebble, while I sat by and smoked. Restful! No—I shouldn't call her a restful personality, exactly. Not to me, at any rate. In the evening she would liven up and talk a little more, but she generally went up to bed early, and left Merridew and me to chat together in the garden.

Oh! about the revolver. Yes. I bought that in Bath, when I had been at Little Hexham exactly a week. We drove over in the morning, and while Mrs. Merridew got some things for her husband, I prowled round the secondhand shops. I had intended to get an air gun or a peashooter or something of that kind, when I saw this. You've seen it, of course. It's very tiny—what people in books describe as "little more than a toy," but quite deadly enough. The old boy who sold it to me didn't seem to know much about firearms. He'd taken it in pawn some time back, he told me, and there were ten rounds of ammunition with it. He made no bones about a license or anything—glad enough to make a sale, no doubt, without putting difficulties in a customer's way. I told him I knew how to handle it, and mentioned by way of a joke that I meant to take a potshot or two at the cats. That seemed to wake him up a bit. He was a dried-up little fellow, with a scrawny gray beard and a stringy neck. He asked me where I was staying. I told him at Little Hexham.

"You better be careful, sir," he said. "They think a heap of their cats down there, and it's reckoned unlucky to kill them." And then he added something I couldn't quite catch, about a silver bullet. He was a doddering old fellow, and he seemed to have some sort of scruple about letting me take the parcel away, but I assured him that I was perfectly capable of looking after it and myself. I left him standing in the door of his shop, pulling at his beard and staring after me.

That night the thunder came. The sky had turned to lead before evening, but the dull heat was more oppressive than the sunshine. Both the Merridews seemed to be in a state of nerves —he sulky and swearing at the weather and the flies, and she wrought up to a queer kind of vivid excitement. Thunder affects some people that way. I wasn't much better, and to make things worse I got the feeling that the house was full of cats. I couldn't see them, but I knew they were there, lurking behind the cupboards and flitting noiselessly about the corridors. I could scarcely sit in the parlor and I was thankful to escape to my room. Cats or no cats I had to open the window, and I sat there with my pajama jacket unbuttoned, trying to get a breath of air. But the place was like the inside of a copper furnace. And pitch-dark. I could scarcely see from my window where the bushes ended and the lawn began. But I could hear and feel the cats. There were little scrapings in the wisteria and scufflings among the leaves, and about eleven o'clock one of them started the concert with a loud and hideous wail. Then another and another joined in—I'll swear there were fifty of them. And presently I got that foul sensation of nausea, and the flesh crawled on my bones, and I knew that one of them was slinking close to me in the darkness. I looked round quickly, and there she stood, the great Cyprian, right against my shoulder, her eyes glowing like green lamps. I yelled and struck out at her, and she snarled as she leaped out and down. I heard her thump the gravel, and the yowling burst out all over the garden with renewed vehemence. And then all in a moment there was utter silence, and in the far distance there came a flickering blue flash and then another. In the first of them I saw the far garden wall, topped all along its length with cats, like a nursery frieze. When the second flash came, the wall was empty.

At two o'clock the rain came. For three hours before that I had sat there, watching the lightning as it spat across the sky and exulting in the crash of the thunder. The storm seemed to carry off all the electrical disturbance in my body; I could have shouted with excitement and relief. The first heavy drops fell, then a steady downpour, then a deluge. It struck the iron-baked garden with a noise like steel rods falling. The smell of the ground came up intoxicatingly, and the wind rose and flung the rain in against my face. At the other end of the passage I heard a window thrown to and fastened, but I leaned out into the tumult and let the water drench my head and shoulders. The thunder still rumbled intermittently, but with less noise and farther off, and in an occasional flash I saw the white grille of falling water drawn between me and the garden.

It was after one of these thunder peals that I became aware of a knocking at my door. I opened it, and there was Merridew. He had a candle in his hand, and his face was terrified.

"Felice!" he said, abruptly. "She's ill. I can't wake her. For God's sake, come and give me a hand." I hurried down the passage after him. There were two beds in his room—a great four-poster, hung with crimson damask, and a small camp bedstead drawn up near to the window. The small bed was empty, the bedclothes tossed aside; evidently he had just risen from it. In the four-poster lay Mrs. Merridew, naked, with only a sheet upon her. She was stretched flat upon her back, her long black hair in two plaits over her shoulders. Her face was waxen and shrunk, like the face of a corpse, and her pulse, when I felt it, was so faint that at first I could scarcely feel it. Her breathing was very slow and shallow, and her flesh cold. I shook her, but there was no response at all. I lifted her eyelids, and noticed how the eyeballs were turned up under the upper lid, so that only the whites were visible. The touch of my fingertip upon the sensitive ball evoked no reaction. I immediately wondered whether she took drugs.

Merridew seemed to think it necessary to make some explanation. He was babbling about the heat—she couldn't bear so much as a silk nightgown—she had suggested that he should occupy the other bed—he had slept heavily—right through the thunder. The rain blowing in on his face had aroused him. He had got up and shut the window. Then he had called to Felice to know if she was all right—he thought the storm might have frightened her. There was no answer. He had struck a light. Her condition had alarmed him—and so on.

I told him to pull himself together and to try, by chafing his wife's hands and feet, to restore the circulation. I had it firmly in my mind that she was under the influence of some opiate. We set to work, rubbing and pinching and slapping her with wet towels and shouting her name in her ear. It was like handling a dead woman, except for the very slight but perfectly regular rise and fall of her bosom, on which—with a kind of surprise that there should be any flaw on its magnolia whiteness—I noticed a large brown mole, just over the heart. To my perturbed fancy it suggested a wound and a menace. We had been hard at it for some time, with the sweat pouring off us, when we became aware of something going on outside the window—a stealthy bumping and scraping against the panes. I snatched up the candle and looked out.

On the sill, the Cyprian cat sat and clawed at the casement. Her drenched fur clung limply to her body, her eyes glared into mine, her mouth was opened in protest. She scrabbled furiously at the latch, her hind claws slipping and scratching on the woodwork. I hammered on the pane and bawled at her, and she struck back at the glass as though possessed. As I cursed her and turned away, she set up a long, despairing wail.

Merridew called to me to bring back the candle and leave the brute alone. I returned to the bed, but the dismal crying went on and on incessantly. I suggested to Merridew that he should wake the landlord and get hot-water bottles and some brandy from the bar and see if a messenger could not be sent for a doctor. He departed on this errand, while I went on with my massage. It seemed to me that the pulse was growing still fainter. Then I suddenly recollected that I had a small brandy flask in my bag. I ran out to fetch it, and as I did so the cat suddenly stopped its howling.

As I entered my own room the air blowing through the open window struck gratefully upon me. I found my bag in the dark and was rummaging for the flask among my shirts and socks when I heard a loud, triumphant meow, and turned round in time to see the Cyprian cat crouched for a moment on the sill, before it sprang in past me and out at the door. I found the flask and hastened back with it, just as Merridew and the landlord came running up the stairs.

We all went into the room together. As we did so, Mrs. Merridew stirred, sat up and asked us what in the world was the matter.

I have seldom felt quite such a fool.

Next day the weather was cooler; the storm had cleared the air. What Merridew had said to his wife I do not know. None of us made any public allusion to the night's disturbance, and to all appearance Mrs. Merridew was in the best of health and spirits. Merridew took a day off from the waterworks, and we all went for a long drive and picnic together. We were on the best of terms with one another. Ask Merridew—he will tell you the same thing. He would not—he could not, surely—say otherwise. I can't believe, Harringay, I simply cannot believe that he could imagine or suspect me—I say, there was nothing to suspect. Nothing.

Yes—this is the important date—the 24th of June. I can't tell you any more details; there is nothing to tell. We came back and had dinner just as usual. All three of us were together all day, till bedtime. On my honor I had no private meeting of any kind that day, either with him or with her. I was the first to go to bed, and I heard the others come upstairs about half an hour later. They were talking cheerfully.

The Cyprian Cat

It was a moonlight night. For once, no caterwauling came to trouble me. I didn't even bother to shut the window or the door. I put the revolver on the chair beside me before I lay down. Yes, it was loaded. I had no special object in putting it there, except that I meant to have a go at the cats if they started their games again.

I was desperately tired, and thought I should drop off to sleep at once, but I didn't. I must have been overtired, I suppose. I lay and looked at the moonlight. And then, about midnight, I heard what I had been half expecting: a stealthy scrabbling in the wisteria and a faint meowing sound.

I sat up in bed and reached for the revolver. I heard the *plop* as the big cat sprang up onto the window ledge; I saw her black and silver flanks, and the outline of her round head, pricked ears and upright tail. I aimed and fired, and the beast let out one frightful cry and sprang down into the room.

I jumped out of bed. The crack of the shot had sounded terrific in the silent house, and somewhere I heard a distant voice call out. I pursued the cat into the passage, revolver in hand—with some idea of finishing it off, I suppose. And then, at the door of the Merridew's room, I saw Mrs. Merridew. She stood with one hand on each doorpost, swaying to and fro. Then she fell down at my feet. Her bare breast was all stained with blood. And as I stood staring at her, clutching the revolver, Merridew came out and found us—like that.

Well, Harringay, that's my story, exactly as I told it to Peabody. I'm afraid it won't sound very well in court, but what can I say? The trail of blood led from my room to hers; the cat must have run that way; I *know* it was the cat I shot. I can't offer any explanation. I don't know who shot Mrs. Merridew, or why. I can't help it if the people at the inn say they never saw the Cyprian cat; Merridew saw it that other night, and I know he wouldn't lie about it. Search the house, Harringay—that's the only thing to do. Pull the place to pieces, till you find the body of the Cyprian cat. It will have my bullet in it.

A Haunted Island

ALGERNON BLACKWOOD

THE FOLLOWING EVENTS OCCURRED on a small island of isolated position in a large Canadian lake, to whose cool waters the inhabitants of Montreal and Toronto flee for rest and recreation in the hot months. It is only to be regretted that events of such peculiar interest to the genuine student of the psychic should be entirely uncorroborated. Such, unfortunately, however, is the case.

Our own party of nearly twenty had returned to Montreal that very day, and I was left in solitary possession for a week or two longer, in order to accomplish some important reading for the law, which I had foolishly neglected during the summer.

With a whole island to oneself, a two-story cottage, a canoe, and only the chipmunks and the farmer's weekly visit with eggs and bread to disturb one, the opportunities for hard reading might be very great. It all depends!

The rest of the party had gone off with many warnings to beware of Indians and not to stay late enough to be the victim of a frost that thinks nothing of forty below zero. After they had gone, the loneliness of the situation made itself unpleasantly felt. There were no other islands within six or seven miles, and

A Haunted Island

though the mainland forests lay a couple of miles behind me, they stretched for a very great distance, unbroken by any signs of human habitation. But, though the island was completely deserted and silent, the rocks and trees that had echoed human laughter and voices almost every hour of the day for two months could not fail to retain some memories of it all, and I was not surprised to fancy I heard a shout or a cry as I passed from rock to rock, and more than once to imagine that I heard my own name called aloud.

In the cottage there were six tiny little bedrooms divided from one another by plain unvarnished partitions of pine. A wooden bedstead, a mattress, and a chair stood in each room, but I only found two mirrors, and one of these was broken.

The boards creaked a good deal as I moved about, and the signs of occupation were so recent that I could hardly believe I was alone. I half expected to find someone left behind, still trying to crowd into a box more than it would hold. The door of one room was stiff and refused for a moment to open, and it required very little persuasion to imagine someone was holding the handle on the inside, and that when it opened, I should meet a pair of human eyes.

A thorough search of the floor led me to select as my own sleeping quarters a little room with a diminutive balcony over the veranda roof. The room was very small, but the bed was large and had the best mattress of them all. It was situated directly over the sitting room where I should live and do my reading, and the miniature window looked out to the rising sun. With the exception of a narrow path which led from the front door and veranda through the trees to the boat landing, the island was densely covered with maples, hemlocks, and cedars. The trees gathered in around the cottage so closely that the slightest wind made the branches scrape the roof and tap the wooden walls. A few moments after sunset the darkness became impenetrable, and ten yards beyond the glare of the lamps that shone through the sitting-room windows—of which there were six—you could not see an inch beyond your nose, nor move a step without running up against a tree.

The rest of that day I spent moving my belongings from my tent to the sitting room, taking stock of the contents of the larder, and chopping enough wood for the stove to last me for a week. After that, just before sunset, I went round the island a couple of times in my canoe for precaution's sake. I had never dreamed of doing this before, but when a man is alone, he does things that never occur to him when he is one of a large party.

How lonely the island seemed when I landed again! The sun was down, and twilight is unknown in these northern regions. The darkness comes up at once. The canoe safely pulled up and turned over on her face, I groped my way up the little narrow pathway to the veranda. The six lamps were soon burning merrily in the front room, but in the kitchen, where I dined, the shadows were so gloomy, and the lamplight was so inadequate, that the stars could be seen peeping through the cracks between the rafters.

I turned in early that night. Though it was calm and there was no wind, the creaking of my bedstead and the musical gurgle of the water over the rocks below were not the only sounds that reached my ears. As I lay awake, the appalling emptiness of the house grew upon me. The corridors and vacant rooms seemed to echo innumerable footsteps, shufflings, the rustle of skirts, and a constant undertone of whispering. When sleep at length overtook me, the breathings and noises, however, passed gently to mingle with the voices of my dreams.

A week passed by, and the reading progressed favorably. On the tenth day of my solitude, a strange thing happened. I awoke after a good night's sleep to find myself possessed with a marked repugnance for my room. The air seemed to stifle me. The more I tried to define the cause of this dislike, the more unreasonable it appeared. There was something about the room that made me afraid. Absurd as it seems, this feeling clung to me obstinately while dressing, and more than once I caught myself shivering, and conscious of an inclination to get out of the room as quickly as possible. The more I tried to laugh it away, the more real it became, and when at last I was dressed, and went out into the passage, and downstairs into the kitchen, it was with feelings of relief, such as I might imagine would accompany one's escape from the presence of a dangerous contagious disease.

While cooking my breakfast, I carefully recalled every night spent in the room, in the hope that I might in some way connect the dislike I now felt with some disagreeable incident that had occurred in it. But the only thing I could recall was one stormy night when I suddenly awoke and heard the boards creaking so loudly in the corridor that I was convinced there were people in the house. So certain was I of this, that I had descended the stairs, gun in hand, only to find the doors and windows securely fastened, and the mice and cockroaches in sole possession of the floor. This was certainly not sufficient to account for the strength of my feelings.

The morning hours I spent in steady reading, and when I broke off in the middle of the day for a swim and luncheon, I was very much surprised, if not a little alarmed, to find that my dislike for the room had, if anything, grown stronger. Going upstairs to get a book, I experienced the most marked aversion to entering the room, and while within I was conscious all the time of an uncomfortable feeling that was half uneasiness and half apprehension. The result of it was that, instead of reading, I spent the afternoon on the water, paddling and fishing, and when I got home about sundown, brought with me half a dozen delicious black bass for the supper table and the larder.

As sleep was an important matter to me at this time, I had decided that if my aversion to the room was so strongly marked on my return as it had been before, I would move my bed down into the sitting room and sleep there. This was, I argued, in no sense a concession to an absurd and fanciful fear, but simply a precaution to ensure a good night's sleep. A bad night involved the loss of the next day's reading—a loss I was not prepared to incur.

I accordingly moved my bed downstairs into a corner of the

sitting room facing the door, and was moreover uncommonly glad when the operation was completed and the door of the bedroom closed finally upon the shadows, the silence, and the strange *fear* that shared the room with them.

The croaking stroke of the kitchen clock sounded the hour of eight as I finished washing up my few dishes and, closing the kitchen door behind me, passed into the front room. All the lamps were lit, and their reflectors, which I had polished up during the day, threw a blaze of light into the room.

Outside the night was still and warm. Not a breath of air was stirring; the waves were silent, the trees motionless, and heavy clouds hung like an oppressive curtain over the heavens. The darkness seemed to have rolled up with unusual swiftness, and not the faintest glow of color remained to show where the sun had set. There was present in the atmosphere that ominous and overwhelming silence which so often precedes the most violent storms.

I sat down to my books with my brain unusually clear, and in my heart the pleasant satisfaction of knowing that five black bass were lying in the icehouse, and that tomorrow morning the old farmer would arrive with fresh bread and eggs. I was soon absorbed in my books.

As the night wore on, the silence deepened. Even the chipmunks were still, and the boards of the floors and walls ceased creaking. I read on steadily till, from the gloomy shadows of the kitchen, came the hoarse sound of the clock striking nine. How loud the strokes sounded! They were like blows of a big hammer. I closed one book and opened another, feeling that I was just warming up to my work.

This, however, did not last long. I presently found that I was reading the same paragraphs over twice, simple paragraphs that did not require such effort. Then I noticed that my mind began to wander to other things, and the effort to recall my thoughts became harder with each digression. Concentration was growing momentarily more difficult. Presently I discovered that I had turned over two pages instead of one, and had not noticed my mistake until I was well down the page. This was becoming serious. What was the disturbing influence? It could not be physical fatigue. On the contrary, my mind was unusually alert, and in a more receptive condition than usual. I made a new and determined effort to read, and for a short time succeeded in giving my whole attention to my subject. But in a very few moments again I found myself leaning back in my chair, staring vacantly into space.

Something was evidently at work in my subconsciousness. There was something I had neglected to do. Perhaps the kitchen door and windows were not fastened. I accordingly went to see, and found that they were! The fire perhaps needed attention. I went in to see, and found that it was all right! I looked at the lamps, went upstairs into every bedroom in turn, and then went round the house, and even into the icehouse. Nothing was wrong; everything was in its place. Yet something *was* wrong! The conviction grew stronger and stronger within me.

When I at length settled down to my books again and tried to read, I became aware, for the first time, that the room seemed to be growing cold. Yet the day had been oppressively warm, and evening had brought no relief. The six big lamps, moreover, gave out enough heat to warm the room pleasantly. But a chilliness, that perhaps crept up from the lake, made itself felt in the room, and caused me to get up to close the glass door opening onto the veranda.

For a brief moment I stood looking out at the shaft of light that fell from the windows and shone some little distance down the pathway and out for a few feet into the lake.

As I looked I saw a canoe glide into the pathway of light, and immediately crossing it, pass out of sight again into the darkness. It was perhaps a hundred feet from the shore, and it moved swiftly.

I was surprised that a canoe should pass the island at that time of night, for all the summer visitors from the other side of the lake had gone home weeks before, and the island was a long way out of any line of water traffic.

My reading from this moment did not make very good progress, for somehow the picture of that canoe, gliding so dimly and swiftly across the narrow track of light on the black waters, silhouetted itself against the background of my mind with singular vividness. It kept coming between my eyes and the printed page. The more I thought about it, the more surprised I became. It was of larger build than any I had seen during the past summer months, and was more like the old Indian war canoes with the high curving bows and stern and wide beam. The more I tried to read, the less success attended my efforts, and finally I closed my books and went out on the veranda to walk up and down a bit and shake the chilliness out of my bones.

The night was perfectly still, and as dark as imaginable. I stumbled down the path to the little landing wharf, where the water made the very faintest of gurgling under the timbers. The sound of a big tree falling in the mainland forest, far across the lake, stirred echoes in the heavy air, like the first guns of a distant night attack. No other sound disturbed the stillness that reigned supreme.

As I stood upon the wharf in the broad splash of light that followed me from the sitting-room windows, I saw another canoe cross the pathway of uncertain light upon the water and disappear at once into the impenetrable gloom that lay beyond. This time I saw more distinctly than before. It was like the former canoe, a big birchbark, with high-crested bow and stern and broad beam. It was paddled by two Indians, of whom the one in the stern—the steerer—appeared to be a very large man. I could see this very plainly, and though the second canoe was much nearer the island than the first, I judged that they were both on their way home to the government reservation, which was situated some fifteen miles away upon the mainland.

I was wondering in my mind what could possibly bring any

A Haunted Island

Indians down to this part of the lake at such an hour of the night, when a third canoe, of precisely similar build, and also occupied by two Indians, passed silently round the end of the wharf. This time the canoe was very much nearer shore, and it suddenly flashed into my mind that the three canoes were in reality one and the same, and that only one canoe was circling the island!

This was by no means a pleasant reflection, because, if it were the correct solution of the unusual appearance of the three canoes in this lonely part of the lake at so late an hour, the purpose of the two men could only reasonably be considered to be in some way connected with myself. I had never known of the Indians attempting any violence upon the settlers who shared the wild, inhospitable country with them; at the same time, it was not beyond the region of possibility to suppose . . . But then I did not care even to think of such hideous possibilities, and my imagination immediately sought relief in all manner of other solutions to the problem, which indeed came readily enough to my mind, but did not succeed in recommending themselves to my reason.

Meanwhile, by a sort of instinct, I stepped back out of the bright light in which I had hitherto been standing, and waited in the deep shadow of a rock to see if the canoe would again make its appearance. Here I could see, without being seen, and the precaution seemed a wise one.

After less than five minutes, the canoe, as I had anticipated, made its fourth appearance. This time it was not twenty yards from the wharf, and I saw that the Indians meant to land. I recognized the two men as those who had passed before, and the steerer was certainly an immense fellow. It was unquestionably the same canoe. There could no longer be any doubt that for some purpose of their own the men had been going round and round the island for some time, waiting for an opportunity to land. I strained my eyes to follow them in the darkness, but the night had completely swallowed them up, and not even the faintest swish of the paddles reached my ears as the Indians plied their long and powerful strokes. The canoe would be round again in a few moments, and this time it was possible that the men might land. It was well to be prepared. I knew nothing of their intentions, and two to one (when the two are big Indians!) late at night on a lonely island was not exactly my idea of a pleasant encounter.

In a corner of the sitting room, leaning up against the back wall, stood my Marlin rifle, with ten cartridges in the magazine and one lying snugly in the greased breech. There was just time to get up to the house and take up a position of defense in that corner. Without an instant's hesitation I ran up to the veranda, carefully picking my way among the trees, so as to avoid being seen in the light. Entering the room, I shut the door leading to the veranda, and as quickly as possible turned out every one of the six lamps. To be in a room so brilliantly lit, where my every movement could be observed from outside, while I could see nothing but impenetrable darkness at every window, was by all laws of warfare an unnecessary concession to the enemy. And this enemy, if enemy it was to be, was far too wily and dangerous to be granted any such advantages.

I stood in the corner of the room with my back against the wall, and my hand on the cold rifle barrel. The table, covered with my books, lay between me and the door, but for the first few minutes after the lights were out, the darkness was so intense that nothing could be discerned at all. Then, very gradually, the outline of the room became visible, and the framework of the windows began to shape itself dimly before my eyes.

After a few minutes the door (its upper half of glass) and the two windows that looked out upon the front veranda became especially distinct, and I was glad that this was so, because if the Indians came up to the house, I should be able to see their approach and gather something of their plans. Nor was I mistaken, for there presently came to my ears the peculiar hollow sound of a canoe landing and being carefully dragged up over the rocks. The paddles I distinctly heard being placed under-

A Haunted Island

neath, and the silence that ensued thereupon I rightly interpreted to mean that the Indians were stealthily approaching the house....

While it would be absurd to claim that I was not alarmed—even frightened—at the gravity of the situation and its possible outcome, I speak the whole truth when I say that I was not overwhelmingly afraid for myself. I was conscious that even at this stage of the night I was passing into a psychic condition in which my sensations seemed no longer normal. Physical fear at no time entered into the nature of my feelings, and though I kept my hand upon my rifle the greater part of the night, I was all the time conscious that its assistance could be of little avail against the terrors that I had to face. More than once I seemed to feel most curiously that I was in no real sense a part of the proceedings, nor actually involved in them, but that I was playing the part of a spectator—a spectator, moreover, on a psychic rather than on a material plane. Many of my sensations that night were too vague for definite description and analysis, but the main feeling that will stay with me to the end of my days is the awful horror of it all, and the miserable sensation that if the strain had lasted a little longer than was actually the case, my mind must inevitably have given way.

Meanwhile I stood still in my corner, and waited patiently for what was to come. The house was as still as the grave, but the inarticulate voices of the night sang in my ears, and I seemed to hear the blood running in my veins and dancing in my pulses.

If the Indians came to the back of the house, they would find the kitchen door and window securely fastened. They could not get in there without making considerable noise, which I was bound to hear. The only mode of getting in was by means of the door that faced me, and I kept my eyes glued on that door without taking them off for the smallest fraction of a second.

My sight adapted itself every minute better to the darkness. I saw the table that nearly filled the room and left only a narrow passage on each side. I could also make out the straight backs of the wooden chairs pressed up against it, and could even distinguish my papers and inkstand lying on the white oilcloth covering. I thought of the gay faces that had gathered round that table during the summer, and I longed for the sunlight as I had never longed for it before.

Less than three feet to my left, the passageway led to the kitchen, and the stairs leading to the bedrooms above commenced in the passageway but almost in the sitting room itself. Through the windows I could see the dim motionless outlines of the trees: not a leaf stirred, not a branch moved.

A few moments of this awful silence, and then I was aware of a soft tread on the boards of the veranda, so stealthy that it seemed an impression directly on my brain rather than upon the nerves of hearing. Immediately afterward a black figure darkened the glass door, and I perceived that a face was pressed against the upper panes. A shiver ran down my back, and my hair was conscious of a tendency to rise and stand at right angles to my head.

It was the figure of an Indian, broad-shouldered and immense —indeed, the largest figure of a man I have ever seen outside of a circus hall. By some power of light that seemed to generate itself in the brain, I saw the strong dark face with the aquiline nose and high cheekbones flattened against the glass. The direction of the gaze I could not determine, but faint gleams of light as the big eyes rolled round and showed their whites told me plainly that no corner of the room escaped their searching.

For what seemed fully five minutes, the dark figure stood there, with the huge shoulders bent forward so as to bring the head down to the level of the glass; while behind him, though not nearly so large, the shadowy form of the other Indian swayed to and fro like a bent tree. While I waited in an agony of suspense and agitation for their next movement, little currents of icy sensation ran up and down my spine, and my heart seemed alternately to stop beating and then start up again with terrifying rapidity. They must have heard its thumping and the singing of the blood in my head! Moreover, I was conscious, as I felt a cold stream of perspiration trickle down my face, of a desire to scream, to shout, to bang the walls like a child, to make a noise, or do anything that would relieve the suspense and bring things to a speedy climax.

It was probably this inclination that led me to another discovery, for when I tried to bring my rifle from behind my back to raise it and have it pointed at the door ready to fire, I found that I was powerless to move. The muscles, paralyzed by this strange fear, refused to obey the will. Here indeed was a terrifying complication!

There was a faint sound of rattling at the brass knob, and the door was pushed open a couple of inches. A pause of a few seconds, and it was pushed open still further. Without a sound of footsteps that was appreciable to my ears, the two figures glided into the room, and the man behind gently closed the door after him.

They were alone with me between four walls. Could they see me standing there, so still and straight in my corner? Had they, perhaps, already seen me? My blood surged and sang like the rolls of drums in an orchestra, and though I did my best to suppress my breathing, it sounded like the rushing of wind through a pneumatic tube.

My suspense as to the next move was soon at an end—only, however, to give place to a new and keener alarm. The men had hitherto exchanged no words and no signs, but there were general indications of a movement across the room, and whichever way they went, they would have to pass round the table. If they came my way, they would have to pass within six inches of my person. While I was considering this very disagreeable possibility, I perceived that the smaller Indian (smaller by comparison) suddenly raised his arm and pointed to the ceiling. The other fellow raised his head and followed the direction of his companion's arm. I began to understand at last. They were going upstairs, and the room directly overhead to which they pointed had been until this night my bedroom. It was the room in which I had experienced that very morning so strange a sensation of fear, and but for which I should then have been lying asleep in the narrow bed against the window.

The Indians then began to move silently around the room; they were going upstairs, and they were coming around my side of the table. So stealthy were their movements that, but for the abnormally sensitive state of the nerves, I should never have heard them. As it was, their catlike tread was distinctly audible. Like two monstrous black cats they came round the table toward me, and for the first time I perceived that the smaller of the two dragged something along the floor behind him. As it trailed along over the floor with a soft, sweeping sound, I somehow got the impression that it was a large dead thing with outstretched wings, or a large, spreading cedar branch. Whatever it was, I was unable to see it even in outline, and I was too terrified, even had I possessed the power over my muscles, to move my neck forward in the effort to determine its nature.

Nearer and nearer they came. The leader rested a giant hand upon the table as he moved. My lips were glued together, and the air seemed to burn in my nostrils. I tried to close my eyes, so that I might not see as they passed me, but my eyelids had stiffened and refused to obey. Would they never get by me? Sensation seemed also to have left my legs, and it was as if I were standing on mere supports of wood or stone. Worse still, I was conscious that I was losing the power of balance, the power to stand upright, or even to lean backward against the wall. Some force was drawing me forward, and a dizzy terror seized me that I should lose my balance and topple forward against the Indians just as they were in the act of passing me.

Even moments drawn out into hours must come to an end sometime, and almost before I knew it the figures had passed me and had their feet upon the lowest step of the stairs leading to the upper bedrooms. There could not have been six inches between us, and yet I was conscious only of a current of cold air that followed them. They had not touched me, and I was convinced that they had not seen me. Even the trailing thing on the floor behind them had not touched my feet, as I had dreaded it would, and on such an occasion as this I was grateful even for the smallest mercies.

The absence of the Indians from my immediate neighborhood brought little sense of relief. I stood shivering and shuddering in my corner, and, beyond being able to breathe more freely, I felt no whit less uncomfortable. Also, I was aware that a certain light, which, without apparent source or rays, had enabled me to follow their every gesture and movement, had gone out of the room with their departure. An unnatural darkness filled the room and pervaded its every corner so that I could barely make out the positions of the windows and the glass doors.

As I said before, my condition was evidently an abnormal one. The capacity for feeling surprise seemed, as in dreams, to be wholly absent. My senses recorded with unusual accuracy every smallest occurrence, but I was able to draw only the simplest deductions.

The Indians soon reached the top of the stairs, and there they halted for a moment. I had not the faintest clue as to their next movement. They appeared to hesitate. They were listening attentively. Then I heard one of them, who by the weight of his soft tread must have been the giant, cross the narrow corridor and enter the room directly overhead—my own little bedroom. But for the insistence of that unaccountable dread I had experienced there in the morning, I should at that very moment have been lying in the bed with the big Indian in the room standing beside me.

For a space of a hundred seconds, there was silence, such as might have existed before the birth of sound. It was followed by a long quivering shriek of terror, which rang out into the night and ended in a short gulp before it had run its full course. At the same moment the other Indian left his place at the head of the stairs and joined his companion in the bedroom. I heard the "thing" trailing behind him along the floor. A thud followed, as of something heavy falling, and then all became still and silent as before.

It was at this point that the atmosphere, surcharged all day with the electricity of a fierce storm, found relief in a dancing flash of brilliant lightning simultaneously with a crash of loudest thunder. For five seconds every article in the room was visible to me with amazing distinctness, and through the windows I saw the tree trunks standing in solemn rows. The thunder pealed and echoed across the lake and among the distant islands, and the floodgates of heaven then opened and let out their rain in streaming torrents.

The drops fell with a swift rushing sound upon the still waters of the lake, which leaped up to meet them, and pattered with the rattle of shot on the leaves of the maples and the roof of the cottage. A moment later, and another flash, even more brilliant and of longer duration than the first, lit up the sky from zenith to horizon, and bathed the room momentarily in dazzling whiteness. I could see the rain glistening on the leaves and branches outside. The wind rose suddenly, and in less than a minute the storm that had been gathering all day burst forth in its full fury.

Above all the noisy voices of the elements, the slightest sounds in the room overhead made themselves heard, and in the few seconds of deep silence that followed the shriek of terror and pain, I was aware that the movements had commenced again. The men were leaving the room and approaching the top of the stairs. A short pause, and they began to descend. Behind them, tumbling from step to step, I could hear that trailing "thing" being dragged along. It had become ponderous!

I awaited their approach with a degree of calmness, almost of apathy, which was only explicable on the ground that after a certain point Nature applies her own anesthetic, and a merciful condition of numbness supervenes. On they came, step by step, nearer and nearer, with the shuffling sound of the burden behind growing louder as they approached.

A Haunted Island

They were already halfway down the stairs when I was galvanized afresh into a condition of terror by the consideration of a new and horrible possibility. It was the reflection that if another vivid flash of lightning were to come when the shadowy procession was in the room, perhaps when it was actually passing in front of me, I should see everything in detail, and worse, be seen myself! I could only hold my breath and wait—wait while the minutes lengthened into hours, and the procession made its slow progress around the room.

The Indians had reached the foot of the staircase. The form of the huge leader loomed in the doorway of the passage, and the burden, with an ominous thud, had dropped from the last step to the floor. There was a moment's pause while I saw the Indian turn and stoop to assist his companion. Then the procession moved forward again, entered the room close on my left, and began to move slowly round my side of the table. The leader was already beyond me, and his companion, dragging on the floor behind him the burden, whose confused outline I could dimly make out, was exactly in front of me, when the cavalcade came to a dead halt. At the same moment, with the strange suddenness of thunderstorms, the splash of the rain ceased altogether, and the wind died away into utter silence.

For the space of five seconds, my heart seemed to stop beating, and then the worst came. A double flash of lightning lit up the room and its contents with merciless vividness.

The huge Indian leader stood a few feet past me on my right. One leg was stretched forward in the act of taking a step. His immense shoulders were turned toward his companion, and in all their magnificent fierceness I saw the outline of his features. His gaze was directed upon the burden his companion was dragging along the floor; but his profile, with the big aquiline nose, high cheekbones, straight black hair, and bold chin, burnt itself in that brief instant into my brain, never again to fade.

Dwarfish, compared with this gigantic figure, appeared the proportions of the other Indian, who, within twelve inches of my face, was stooping over the thing he was dragging in a position that lent to his person the additional horror of deformity. And the burden, lying upon a sweeping cedar branch which he held and dragged by a long stem, was the body of a white man. The scalp had been neatly lifted, and blood lay in a broad smear upon the cheeks and forehead.

Then, for the first time that night, the terror that had paralyzed my muscles and my will lifted its unholy spell from my soul. With a loud cry I stretched out my arms to seize the big Indian by the throat and, grasping only air, tumbled forward unconscious upon the ground.

I had recognized the body, and *the face was my own!*

It was bright daylight when a man's voice recalled me to consciousness. I was lying where I had fallen, and the farmer was standing in the room with the loaves of bread in his hands. The horror of the night was still in my heart, and as the bluff settler helped me to my feet and picked up the rifle which had fallen with me, with many questions and expressions of condolence, I imagine my brief replies were neither self-explanatory nor even intelligible.

That day, after a thorough and fruitless search of the house, I left the island and went over to spend my last ten days with the farmer, and when the time came for me to leave, the necessary reading had been accomplished, and my nerves had completely recovered their balance.

On the day of my departure, the farmer started early in his big boat with my belongings to row to the point, twelve miles distant, where a little steamer ran twice a week for the accommodation of hunters. Late in the afternoon I went off in another direction in my canoe, wishing to see the island once again, where I had been the victim of so strange an experience.

In due course I arrived there and made a tour of the island. I also made a search of the little house, and it was not without a curious sensation in my heart that I entered the little upstairs bedroom. There seemed nothing unusual.

Just after I reembarked, I saw a canoe gliding ahead of me around the curve of the island. A canoe was an unusual sight this time of the year, and this one seemed to have sprung from nowhere. Altering my course a little, I watched it disappear around the next projecting point of rock. It had high curving bows, and there were two Indians in it. I lingered with some excitement, to see if it would appear again around the other side of the island, and in less than five minutes it came into view. There were less than two hundred yards between us, and the Indians, sitting on their haunches, were paddling swiftly in my direction.

I never paddled faster in my life than I did in those next few minutes. When I turned to look again, the Indians had altered their course and were again circling the island.

The sun was sinking behind the forests on the mainland, and the crimson-colored clouds of sunset were reflected in the waters of the lake, when I looked round for the last time and saw the big bark canoe and its two dusky occupants still going round the island. Then the shadows deepened rapidly, the lake grew black, and the night wind blew its first breath in my face as I turned the corner, and a projecting bluff of rock hid from my view both island and canoe.

Gay As Cheese

JOAN AIKEN

MR. POL THE BARBER always wore white overalls. He must have had at least six for everyday. He was snowy white and freshly starched as a daisy, his blue eyes, red face and bulbous nose appearing incongruously over the top of the bib. His shop looked like, and was, a kitchen, roughly adapted to barbering with a mirror, basin and some pictures of beautiful girls on the whitewashed walls. It was a long narrow crack of a room with the copper at one end and a tottering flight of steps at the other, leading down to the street; customers waiting their turn mostly sat on the steps in the sun, risking piles and reading *Men Only.*

Mr. Pol rented his upstairs room to an artist, and in the summertime when the customers had been shaved or trimmed, they sometimes went on up the stairs and bought a view of the harbor, water or oil, or a nice still life. The artist had an unlimited supply of these, which he whipped out with the dexterity of a cardsharp.

Both men loved their professions. When the artist was not painting fourteen-by-ten-inch scenes for the tourists, he was engaged on huge, complicated panels of mermaids and sharks, all mixed up with skulls, roses and cabbages, while Mr. Pol hung over the heads of his customers as if he would have liked to gild them.

Gay As Cheese

"Ah, I'm as gay as cheese this morning," he used to say, bustling into his kitchen with a long, gnomish look at the first head of hair waiting to be shorn. "I'll smarten you up till you're like a new button mushroom."

"Now I'm as bright as a pearl," he would exclaim when the long rays of the early sun felt their way back to the copper with an underwater glimmer.

When Mr. Pol laid hands on a customer's head, he knew more about that man than his mother did at birth, or his sweetheart or confessor—not only his past misdeeds but his future ones, what he had had for breakfast and would have for supper, the name of his dog and the day of his death. This should have made Mr. Pol sad or cynical, but it did not. He remained impervious to his portentous gift. Perhaps this was because the destinies of the inhabitants of a small Cornish town contained nothing very startling, and Mr. Pol's divinings seldom soared higher or lower than a winning wager or a sprained ankle.

He never cut his own hair, and had no need to, for he was as bald as an egg.

"It was my own hair falling out that started me thinking on the matter," he told the artist. "All a man's nature comes out in the way his hair grows. It's like a river—watch the currents and you can tell what it's come through, what sort of fish are in it, how fast it's running, how far to the sea."

The artist grunted. He was squatting on the floor, stretching a canvas, and made no reply. He was a taciturn man who despised the tourists for buying his pink and green views.

Mr. Pol looked down at the top of his head and suddenly gave it an affectionate, rumpling pat, as one might to a large woolly dog.

"Ah, that's a nice head of hair. It's a shame you won't let me get at it."

"And have you knowing when I'm going to eat my last bite of bacon? Not likely."

"I wouldn't *tell* you, my handsome!" said Mr. Pol, very shocked. "I'm not one to go measuring people for their coffins before they're ready to step in. I'm as close as a false tooth. There's Sam now, off his truck, the old ruin; I could tell a thing or two about him, but do I?"

He stumped off down the stairs, letting out a snatch of hymn in his powerful baritone.

"And there's some say," he went on, as he sculpted with his shears around the driver's gray head, "that you can grow turnip from carrot seed under the right moon. Who'd want to do that, I ask you?"

"Shorter around the ears," grumbled Sam, scowling down into the enamel basin.

When the night train from Paddington began to draw down the narrow valley toward the sea town, Brian and Fanny Dexter stood up stiffly from the seats where they had slept and started moving their luggage about. Brian was surly and silent, only remarking that it was damned cold and he hoped he could get a shave and a cup of coffee. Fanny glanced doubtfully at her reflection in the little greenish mirror. A white face and narrow eyes, brilliant from lack of sleep, glanced back at her.

"It'll be fine later," she said hopefully. Brian pulled on a sweater without comment. He looked rough but expensive, like a suede shoe. His thick light hair was beginning to gray, but hardly showed it.

"Lady Ward and Penelope said they'd be getting to Pengelly this week," Brian observed. "We might walk along the cliff path later on and see if they've arrived yet. We can do with some exercise to warm us and they'll be expecting us to call."

"I must do my shopping first. It's early closing, and there's all the food to lay in."

Brian shot her an angry look and she was reminded that although the ice of their marriage seemed at the moment to be bearing up, nevertheless there were frightening depths beneath and it was best not to loiter in doubtful spots.

"It won't take long," she said hurriedly.

"It was just an idea," Brian muttered, bundling up a camel-hair overcoat. "Here we are, thank God."

Gay As Cheese

It was still only nine in the morning. The town was gray and forbidding, tilted steeply down to a white sea. The fleet was out; the streets smelled of fish and emptiness. After they had had coffee, Brian announced that he was going to get his shave.

"I'll do my shopping and meet you," suggested Fanny.

"No you bloody well won't, or you'll wander off for hours and I shall have to walk half over the town looking for you," snapped Brian. "You could do with a haircut yourself, you look like a Scotch terrier."

"All right."

She threaded her way after him between the empty tables of the cafe and across the road into Mr. Pol's shop. Mr. Pol was carefully rearranging his tattered magazines.

"Good morning, my handsome," he cautiously greeted Fanny's jeans and sweater and Eton crop, assessing her as a summer visitor.

"Can you give me a shave and my wife a haircut, please?" cut in Brian briskly.

Mr. Pol looked from one to the other of them.

"I'll just put the kettle on for the shave, sir," he answered, moving leisurely to the inner room, "and then I'll trim the young lady, if you'd like to take a seat in the meanwhile."

Brian preferred to stroll back and lean against the doorpost with his hands in his pockets, while Mr. Pol wreathed Fanny's neck in a spotless towel. Her dark head, narrow as a boy's, was bent forward, and he looked benignly at the swirl of glossy hair, flicked a comb through it, and turned her head gently with the palms of his hands.

As he did so, a shudder like an electric shock ran through him and he started back, the comb between his thumb and forefinger jerking upward like a diviner's rod. Neither of the other two noticed; Brian was looking out into the street and Fanny had her eyes on her hands, which were locked together with white knuckles across a fold of the towel.

After a moment Mr. Pol gingerly placed his palms on the sides of her head with a pretense of smoothing the downy hair above

[97]

the ears, and again the shock ran through him. He looked into the mirror, almost expecting to see fish swimming and seaweed floating around her. Death by drowning, and so soon; he could smell salt water and see her thin arm stretched sideways in the wave.

"Don't waste too much time on her," said Brian, looking at his watch. "She doesn't mind what she looks like."

Fanny glanced up and met Mr. Pol's eyes in the glass. There was such a terrified appeal in her look that his hands closed instinctively on her shoulders and his lips parted to form the words "There, there, my handsome. Never mind," before he saw that her appeal was directed not to him, but to her own reflection's pathetic power to please.

"That's lovely," she said to Mr. Pol with a faint smile, and stood up, shaking the glossy dark tufts off her. She sat on one of his chairs, looking at a magazine while Brian took her place and Mr. Pol fetched his steaming kettle.

"You're visiting the town?" Mr. Pol asked, as he rubbed up the lather on his brush. He felt the need to talk.

"Just come off the night train; we're staying here, yes," Brian said shortly.

"It's a pretty place," Mr. Pol remarked. "Plenty of grand walks if you're young and active."

"We're going along to Pengelly by the cliff path this morning," said Brian.

"Oh, but I thought you only said we *might*—" Fanny began incautiously, and then bit off her words.

Brian shot her a look of such hatred that even Mr. Pol caught it, and scuttled into the next room for another razor.

"For heaven's sake, *will* you stop being so damned negative," Brian muttered to her furiously.

"But the groceries—"

"Oh, to hell with the groceries. We'll eat out. Lady Ward and Penelope will think it most peculiar if we don't call—they know we're here. I suppose you want to throw away a valuable social contact for the sake of a couple of ounces of tea. I can't think why you need to do this perpetual shopping—Penelope never does."

"I only thought—"

"Never mind what you thought."

Mr. Pol came back and finished the shave.

"That's a nice head of hair, sir," he said, running his hands over it professionally. "Do you want a trim at all?"

"No thanks," replied Brian abruptly. "Chap in the Burlington Arcade always does it for me. Anything wrong?"

Mr. Pol was staring at the ceiling above Brian's head in a puzzled way.

"No—no, sir, nothing. Nothing at all. I thought for a moment I saw a bit of rope hanging down, but it must have been fancy." Nevertheless Mr. Pol passed his hand once more above Brian's head with the gesture of someone brushing away cobwebs.

"Will that be all? Thank you, sir. Mind how you go on that path to Pengelly. 'Tis always slippery after the rain and we've had one or two falls of rock this summer; all this damp weather loosens them up."

"We'll be all right, thanks," said Brian, who had been walking out of the door without listening to what Mr. Pol was saying. "Come on, Fanny." He swung up the street with Fanny almost running behind him.

"Have they gone? Damnation, I thought I could sell them a view of the cliffs," said the artist, coming in with a little canvas. "Hullo, something the matter?"

For the barber was standing outside his door and staring in indecision and distress after the two figures, now just taking the turning up to the cliff path.

"No," he said at last, turning heavily back and picking up his broom. "No, I'm as gay as cheese."

And he began sweeping up the feathery tufts of dark hair from his stone floor.

[99]

That Hell-Bound Train

ROBERT BLOCH

WHEN MARTIN WAS A LITTLE BOY, his Daddy was a Railroad Man. He never rode the high iron, but he walked the tracks for the CB&Q, and he was proud of his job. And when he got drunk (which was every night), he sang this old song about "That Hell-Bound Train."

Martin didn't quite remember any of the words, but he couldn't forget the way his Daddy sang them out. And when Daddy made the mistake of getting drunk in the afternoon and got squeezed between a Pennsy tank car and an AT&SF gondola, Martin sort of wondered why the Brotherhood didn't sing the song at his funeral.

After that, things didn't go so good for Martin, but somehow he always recalled Daddy's song. When Mom up and ran off with a traveling salesman from Keokuk (Daddy must have turned over in his grave, knowing she'd done such a thing, and with a *passenger,* too!), Martin hummed the tune to himself every night in the Orphan Home. And after Martin himself ran away, he used to whistle the song at night in the jungles, after the other tramps were asleep.

Martin was on the road for four to five years before he realized

That Hell-Bound Train

he wasn't getting anyplace. Of course he'd tried his hand at a lot of things—picking fruit in Oregon, washing dishes in a Montana hash house—but he just wasn't cut out for seasonal labor or pearl-diving, either. Then he graduated to stealing hubcaps in Denver, and for a while he did pretty well with tires in Oklahoma City, but by the time he'd put in six months on the chain gang down in Alabama, he knew he had no future drifting around this way on his own.

So he tried to get on the railroad like his Daddy had, but they told him times were bad; and between the truckers and the airlines and those fancy new fintails General Motors was making, it looked as if the days of the highballers were just about over.

But Martin couldn't keep away from the railroads. Wherever he traveled, he rode the rods; he'd rather hop a freight heading north in subzero weather than lift his thumb to hitch a ride with a Cadillac headed for Florida. Because Martin was loyal to the memory of his Daddy, and he wanted to be as much like him as possible, come what may. Of course, he couldn't get drunk every night, but whenever he did manage to get hold of a can of Sterno, he'd sit there under a nice warm culvert and think about the old days.

Often as not, he'd hum the song about "That Hell-Bound Train." That was the train the drunks and sinners rode: the gambling men and the grifters, the big-time spenders, the skirt chasers, and all the jolly crew. It would be fun to take a trip in such good company, but Martin didn't like to think of what happened when that train finally pulled into the Depot Way Down Yonder. He didn't figure on spending eternity stoking boilers in Hell, without even a company union to protect him. Still, it would be a lovely ride. If there *was* such a thing as a Hell-Bound Train. Which, of course, there wasn't.

At least Martin didn't *think* there was, until that evening when he found himself walking the tracks heading south, just outside of Appleton Junction. The night was cold and dark, the way November nights are in the Fox River Valley, and he knew he'd have to work his way down to New Orleans for the winter, or maybe even Texas. Somehow he didn't much feel like going, even though he'd heard tell that a lot of those Texans' automobiles had solid gold hubcaps.

No sir, he just wasn't cut out for petty larceny. It was worse than a sin—it was unprofitable, too. Bad enough to do the Devil's work, but then to get such miserable pay on top of it! Maybe he'd better let the Salvation Army convert him.

Martin trudged along, humming Daddy's song, waiting for a rattler to pull out of the Junction behind him. He'd have to catch it—there was nothing else for him to do.

Too bad there wasn't a chance to make a better deal for himself somewhere. Might as well be a rich sinner as a poor sinner. Besides, he had a notion that he could strike a pretty shrewd bargain. He'd thought about it a lot, these past few years, particularly when the Sterno was working. Then his ideas would come on strong, and he could figure a way to rig the setup. But that was all nonsense, of course. He might as well join the gospel shouters and turn into a working stiff like all the rest of the world. No use dreaming dreams; a song was only a song and there was no Hell-Bound Train.

There was only *this* train, rumbling out of the night, roaring toward him along the track from the south.

Martin peered ahead, but his eyes couldn't match his ears, and so far all he could recognize was the sound. It *was* a train, though; he felt the steel shudder and sing beneath his feet.

And yet, how could it be? The next station south was Neenah-Menasha, and there was nothing due out of there for hours.

The clouds were thick overhead, and the field mists rolled like a cold fog in a November midnight. Even so, Martin should have been able to see the headlights as the train rushed on. But there were no lights.

There was only the whistle, screaming out of the black throat of the night. Martin could recognize the equipment of just about any locomotive ever built, but he'd never heard a whistle that sounded like this one. It wasn't signaling; it was screaming like a lost soul.

He stepped to one side, for the train was almost on top of him now, and suddenly there it was, looming along the tracks and grinding to a stop in less time than he'd ever believed possible. The wheels hadn't been oiled, because they screamed too, screamed like the damned. But the train slid to a halt and the screams died away into a series of low, groaning sounds, and Martin looked up and saw that this was a passenger train. It was big and black, without a single light shining in the engine cab or any of the long string of cars, and Martin couldn't read any lettering on the sides, but he was pretty sure this train didn't belong on the Northwestern Road.

He was even more sure when he saw the man clamber down out of the forward car. There was something wrong about the way he walked, as though one of his feet dragged. And there was something even more disturbing about the lantern he carried, and what he did with it. The lantern was dark, and when the man alighted, he held it up to his mouth and blew. Instantly the lantern glowed redly. You don't have to be a member of the Railway Brotherhood to know that this is a mighty peculiar way of lighting a lantern.

As the figure approached, Martin recognized the conductor's cap perched on his head, and this made him feel a little better for a moment—until he noticed that it was worn a bit too high, as though there might be something sticking up on the forehead underneath it.

Still, Martin knew his manners, and when the man smiled at him, he said, "Good evening, Mr. Conductor."

"Good evening, Martin."

"How did you know my name?"

The man shrugged. "How did you know I was the conductor?"

"You *are,* aren't you?"

"To you, yes. Although other people, in other walks of life, may recognize me in different roles. For instance, you ought to see what I look like to the folks out in Hollywood." The man grinned. "I travel a great deal," he explained.

"What brings you here?" Martin asked.

"Why, you ought to know the answer to that, Martin. I came because you needed me."

"I did?"

"Don't play the innocent. Ordinarily, I seldom bother with single individuals anymore. The way the world is going, I can expect to carry a full load of passengers without soliciting business. Your name has been down on the list for several years already—I reserved a seat for you as a matter of course. But then, tonight, I suddenly realized you were backsliding. Thinking of joining the Salvation Army, weren't you?"

"Well—" Martin hesitated.

"Don't be ashamed. To err is human, as somebody-or-other once said. *Reader's Digest,* wasn't it? Never mind. The point is, I felt you needed me. So I switched over and came your way."

"What for?"

"Why, to offer you a ride, of course. Isn't it better to travel comfortably by train than to march along the cold streets behind a Salvation Army band? Hard on the feet, they tell me, and even harder on the eardrums."

"I'm not sure I'd care to ride your train, sir," Martin said. "Considering where I'm likely to end up."

"Ah, yes. The old argument." The conductor sighed. "I suppose you'd prefer some sort of bargain, is that it?"

"Exactly," Martin answered.

"Well, I'm afraid I'm all through with that sort of thing. As I mentioned before, times have changed. There's no shortage of prospective passengers anymore. Why should I offer you any special inducements?"

"You must want me, or else you wouldn't have bothered to go out of your way to find me."

The conductor sighed again. "There you have a point. Pride

That Hell-Bound Train

was always my besetting weakness, I admit. And somehow I'd hate to lose you to the competition, after thinking of you as my own all these years." He hesitated. "Yes, I'm prepared to deal with you on your own terms, if you insist."

"The terms?" Martin asked.

"Standard proposition. Anything you want."

"Ah," said Martin.

"But I warn you in advance, there'll be no tricks. I'll grant you any wish you can name—but in return, you must promise to ride the train when the time comes."

"Suppose it never comes?"

"It will."

"Suppose I've got the kind of a wish that will keep me off forever?"

"There *is* no such wish."

"Don't be too sure."

"Let me worry about that," the conductor told him. "No matter what you have in mind, I warn you that I'll collect in the end. And there'll be none of this last-minute hocus-pocus, either. No last-hour repentances, no blonde *Fräuleins* or fancy lawyers showing up to get you off. I offer a clean deal. That is to say, you'll get what you want, and I'll get what I want."

"I've heard you trick people. They say you're worse than a used-car salesman."

"Now wait a minute—"

"I apologize," Martin said, hastily. "But it *is* supposed to be a fact that you can't be trusted."

"I admit it. On the other hand, you seem to think you have found a way out."

"A surefire proposition."

"Surefire? Very funny!" The man began to chuckle, then halted. "But we waste valuable time, Martin. Let's get down to cases. What do you want from me?"

"A single wish."

"Name it and I shall grant it."

[105]

"Anything, you said?"

"Anything at all."

"Very well, then." Martin took a deep breath. "I want to be able to stop Time."

"Right now?"

"No. Not yet. And not for everybody. I realize that would be impossible, of course. But I want to be able to stop Time for myself. Just once, in the future. Whenever I get to a point where I know I'm happy and contented, that's where I'd like to stop. So I can just keep on being happy forever."

"That's quite a proposition," the conductor mused. "I've got to admit I've never heard anything just like it before—and believe me, I've listened to some lulus in my day." He grinned at Martin. "You've really been thinking about this, haven't you?"

"For years," Martin admitted. Then he coughed. "Well, what do you say?"

"It's not impossible in terms of your own *subjective* time sense," the conductor murmured. "Yes, I think it could be arranged."

"But I mean *really* to stop. Not for me just to *imagine* it."

"I understand. And it can be done."

"Then you'll agree?"

"Why not? I promised you, didn't I? Give me your hand."

Martin hesitated. "Will it hurt very much? I mean, I don't like the sight of blood, and—"

"Nonsense! You've been listening to a lot of poppycock. We already have made our bargain, my boy. No need for a lot of childish rigamarole. I merely intend to put something into your hand. The ways and means of fulfilling your wish. After all, there's no telling at just what moment you may decide to exercise the agreement, and I can't drop everything and come running. So it's better to regulate matters for yourself."

"You're going to give me a time stopper?"

"That's the general idea. As soon as I can decide what would be practical." The conductor hesitated. "Ah, the very thing! Here, take my watch."

That Hell-Bound Train

He pulled it out of his vest pocket: a railroad watch in a silver case. He opened the back and made a delicate adjustment; Martin tried to see just exactly what he was doing, but the fingers moved in a blinding blur.

"There we are," the conductor smiled. "It's all set, now. When you finally decide where you'd like to call a halt, merely turn the stem in reverse and unwind the watch until it stops. When it stops, Time stops, for you. Simple enough?"

"Sure thing."

"Then, here, take it." And the conductor dropped the watch into Martin's hand.

The young man closed his fingers tightly around the case. "That's all there is to it, eh?"

"Absolutely. But remember—you can stop the watch only once. So you'd better make sure that you're satisfied with the moment you choose to prolong. I caution you in all fairness; make very certain of your choice."

"I will." Martin grinned. "And since you've been so fair about it, I'll be fair, too. There's one thing you seem to have forgotten. It doesn't really matter *what* moment I choose. Because once I stop Time for myself, that means I stay where I am forever. I'll never have to get any older. And if I don't get any older, I'll never die. And if I never die, then I'll never have to take a ride on your train."

The conductor turned away. His shoulders shook convulsively, and he may have been crying. "And you said *I* was worse than a used-car salesman," he gasped, in a strangled voice.

Then he wandered off into the fog, and the train whistle gave an impatient shriek, and all at once it was moving swiftly down the track, rumbling out of sight in the darkness. Martin stood there, blinking down at the silver watch in his hand. If it wasn't that he could actually see it and feel it there, and if he couldn't smell that peculiar odor, he might have thought he'd imagined the whole thing from start to finish—train, conductor, bargain, and all.

But he had the watch, and he could recognize the scent left by the train as it departed, even though there aren't many locomotives around that use sulphur and brimstone as fuel.

And he had no doubts about his bargain. Better still, he had no doubts as to the advantages of the pact he'd made. That's what came of thinking things through to a logical conclusion. Some fools would have settled for wealth, or power, or Kim Novak. Daddy might have sold out for a fifth of whiskey.

Martin knew that he'd made a better deal. Better? It was foolproof. All he needed to do now was choose his moment. And when the right time came, it was his—forever.

He put the watch in his pocket and started back down the railroad track. He hadn't really had a destination in mind before, but he did now. He was going to find a moment of happiness. . . .

Now young Martin wasn't altogether a ninny. He realized perfectly well that happiness is a relative thing; there are conditions and degrees of contentment, and they vary with one's lot in life. As a hobo, he was often satisfied with a warm handout, a double-length bench in the park, or a can of Sterno made in 1957 (a vintage year). Many a time he had reached a state of momentary bliss through such simple agencies, but he was aware that there were better things. Martin determined to seek them out.

Within two days he was in the great city of Chicago. Quite naturally, he drifted over to West Madison Street, and there he took steps to elevate his role in life. He became a city bum, a panhandler, a moocher. Within a week he had risen to the point where happiness was a meal in a regular one-arm luncheon joint, a two-bit flop on a real army cot in a real flophouse, and a full fifth of muscatel.

There was a night, after enjoying all three of these luxuries to the full, when Martin was tempted to unwind his watch at the pinnacle of intoxication. Then he remembered the faces of the honest johns he'd braced for a handout today. Sure, they were squares, but they were prosperous. They wore good clothes, held good jobs, drove nice cars. And for them, happiness was even more ecstatic: They ate dinner in fine hotels, they slept on innerspring mattresses, they drank blended whiskey.

Squares or no, they *had* something there. Martin fingered his watch, put aside the temptation to hock it for another bottle of muscatel, and went to sleep determining to get himself a job and improve his happiness quotient.

When he awoke he had a hangover, but the determination was still with him. It stayed long after the hangover disappeared, and before the month was out Martin found himself working for a general contractor over on the South Side, at one of the big rehabilitation projects. He hated the grind, but the pay was good, and pretty soon he got himself a one-room apartment out on Blue Island Avenue. He was accustomed to eating in decent restaurants now, and he bought himself a comfortable bed, and every Saturday night he went down to the corner tavern. It was all very pleasant, but—

The foreman liked his work and promised him a raise in a month. If he waited around, the raise would mean that he could even start picking up a girl for a date now and then. Lots of the other fellows on the job did, and they seemed pretty happy.

So Martin kept on working, and the raise came through and the car came through and pretty soon a couple of girls came along.

The first time it happened, he wanted to unwind his watch immediately. Until he got to thinking about what some of the older men always said. There was a guy named Charlie, for example, who worked alongside him on the hoist. "When you're young and don't know the score, maybe you get a kick out of running around with those pigs. But after a while, you want something better. A nice girl of your own. That's the ticket."

Well, he might have something there. At least, Martin owed it to himself to find out. If he didn't like it better, he could always go back to what he had.

It was worth a try. Of course, nice girls don't grow on trees (if they did, a lot more men would become forest rangers), and almost six months went by before Martin met Lillian Gillis. By that time he'd had another promotion and was working inside, in the office. They made him go to night school to learn how to do simple bookkeeping, but it meant another fifteen bucks extra a week, and it was nicer working indoors.

And Lillian *was* a lot of fun. When she told him she'd marry him, Martin was almost sure that the time was now. Except that she was sort of—well, she was a *nice* girl, and she said they'd have to wait until they were married. Of course, Martin couldn't expect to marry her until he had a little money saved up, and another raise would help, too.

That took a year. Martin was patient, because he knew it was going to be worth it. Every time he had any doubts, he took out his watch and looked at it. But he never showed it to Lillian, or anybody else. Most of the other men wore expensive wristwatches and the old silver railroad watch looked just a little cheap.

Martin smiled as he gazed at the stem. Just a few twists and he'd have something none of these other poor working slobs would ever have. Permanent satisfaction, with his blushing bride—

Only getting married turned out to be just the beginning. Sure, it was wonderful, but Lillian told him how much better things would be if they could move into a new place and fix it up. Martin wanted decent furniture, a TV set, a nice car.

So he started taking night courses and got a promotion to the front office. With the baby coming, he wanted to stick around and see his son arrive. And when it came, he realized he'd have to wait until it got a little older, started to walk and talk and develop a personality of its own.

About this time the company sent him out on the road as a troubleshooter on some of those other jobs, and now *he* was eating at those good hotels, living high on the hog and the expense account. More than once he was tempted to unwind his watch. This was the good life. And he realized it could be even better if he just didn't have to *work*. Sooner or later, if he could cut in on one of the company deals, he could make a pile and retire. Then everything would be ideal.

It happened, but it took time. Martin's son was going to high school before he really got up there into the chips. Martin got the feeling that it was now or never, because he wasn't exactly a kid anymore.

But right about then he met Sherry Westcott, and she didn't seem to think he was middle-aged at all, in spite of the way he was losing hair and adding stomach. She taught him that a toupee could cover the bald spot and a cummerbund could cover the potbelly. In fact, she taught him quite a number of things, and he so enjoyed learning that he actually took out his watch and prepared to unwind it.

Unfortunately, he chose the very moment that the private detectives broke down the door of the hotel room, and then there was a long stretch of time when Martin was so busy fighting the divorce action that he couldn't honestly say he was enjoying any given amount.

When he made the final settlement with Lil, he was broke again, and Sherry didn't seem to think he was so young, after all. So he squared his shoulders and went back to work.

He made his pile, eventually, but it took longer this time, and there wasn't much chance to have fun along the way. The fancy dames in the fancy cocktail lounges didn't seem to interest him anymore, and neither did the liquor. Besides, the Doc had warned him about that.

But there were other pleasures for a rich man to investigate. Travel, for instance—and not riding the rods from one hick burg to another, either. Martin went around the world via plane and luxury liner. For a while it seemed as though he would find his moment after all. Visiting the Taj Mahal by moonlight, the moon's radiance was reflected from the back of the battered old watchcase, and Martin got ready to unwind it. Nobody else was there to watch him—

And that's why he hesitated. Sure, this was an enjoyable moment, but he was alone. Lil and the kid were gone, Sherry was gone, and somehow he'd never had time to make any friends. Maybe if he found a few congenial people, he'd have the ultimate happiness. That must be the answer—it wasn't just money or power or sex or seeing beautiful things. The real satisfaction lay in friendship.

So on the boat trip home, Martin tried to strike up a few acquaintances at the ship's bar. But all these people were so much younger, and Martin had nothing in common with them. Also, they wanted to dance and drink, and Martin wasn't in condition to appreciate such pastimes. Nevertheless, he tried.

Perhaps that's why he had the little accident the day before they docked in San Francisco. "Little accident" was the ship's doctor's way of describing it, but Martin noticed he looked very grave when he told him to stay in bed, and he'd called an ambulance to meet the liner at the dock and take the patient right to the hospital.

At the hospital, all the expensive treatment and expensive smiles and expensive words didn't fool Martin any. He was an old man with a bad heart, and they thought he was going to die.

But he could fool them. He still had the watch. He found it in his coat when he put on his clothes and sneaked out of the hospital before dawn.

He didn't have to die. He could cheat death with a single gesture—and he intended to do it as a free man, out there under a free sky.

That was the real secret of happiness. He understood it now. Not even friendship meant as much as freedom. This was the best thing of all—to be free of friends or family or the furies of the flesh.

Martin walked slowly beside the embankment under the night sky. Come to think of it, he was just about back where he'd

That Hell-Bound Train

started, so many years ago. But the moment was good, good enough to prolong forever. Once a bum, always a bum.

He smiled as he thought about it, and then the smile twisted sharply and suddenly, like the pain twisting sharply and suddenly in his chest. The world began to spin and he fell down on the side of the embankment.

He couldn't see very well, but he was still conscious, and he knew what had happened. Another stroke, and a bad one. Maybe this was it. Except that he wouldn't be a fool any longer. He wouldn't wait to see what was still around the corner.

Right now was his chance to use his power and save his life. And he was going to do it. He could still move, nothing could stop him.

He groped in his pocket and pulled out the old silver watch, fumbling with the stem. A few twists and he'd cheat death, he wouldn't have to ride That Hell-Bound Train. He could go on forever.

Forever.

Martin had never really considered the word before. To go on forever—but *how*? Did he *want* to go on forever, like this: a sick old man, lying helplessly here in the grass?

No. He couldn't do it. He wouldn't do it. And suddenly he wanted very much to cry, because he knew that somewhere along the line he'd outsmarted himself. And now it was too late. His eyes dimmed, there was this roaring in his ears. . . .

He recognized the roaring, of course, and he wasn't at all surprised to see the train come rushing out of the fog up there on the embankment. He wasn't surprised when it stopped, either, or when the conductor climbed off and walked slowly toward him.

The conductor hadn't changed a bit. Even his grin was still the same.

"Hello, Martin," he said. "All aboard."

"I know," Martin whispered. "But you'll have to carry me. I can't walk. I'm not even really talking anymore, am I?"

"Yes you are," the conductor said. "I can hear you fine. And you can walk, too." He leaned down and placed his hand on Martin's chest. There was a moment of icy numbness, and then, sure enough, Martin could walk after all.

He got up and followed the conductor along the slope, moving to the side of the train.

"In here?" he asked.

"No, the next car," the conductor murmured. "I guess you're entitled to ride Pullman. After all, you're quite a successful man. You've tasted the joys of wealth and position and prestige. You've known the pleasures of marriage and fatherhood. You've sampled the delights of dining and drinking and debauchery, too, and you traveled high, wide, and handsome. So let's not have any last-minute recriminations."

"All right," Martin sighed. "I guessed I can't blame you for my mistakes. On the other hand, you can't take credit for what happened either. I worked for everything I got. I did it all on my own. I didn't even need your watch."

"So you didn't," the conductor said, smiling. "But would you mind giving it back to me now?"

"Need it for the next sucker, eh?" Martin muttered.

"Perhaps."

Something about the way he said it made Martin look up. He tried to see the conductor's eyes, but the brim of his cap cast a shadow. So Martin looked down at the watch instead, as if seeking an answer there.

"Tell me something," he said, softly. "If I give you the watch, what will you do with it?"

"Why, throw it into the ditch," the conductor told him. "That's all I'll do with it." And he held out his hand.

"What if somebody comes along and finds it? And twists the stem backward, and stops Time?"

"Nobody would do that," the conductor murmured. "Even if they knew."

"You mean, it was all a trick? This is only an ordinary cheap watch?"

That Hell-Bound Train

"I didn't say that," whispered the conductor. "I only said that no one has ever twisted the stem backward. They've all been like you, Martin—looking ahead to find that perfect happiness. Waiting for the moment that never comes."

The conductor held out his hand again.

Martin sighed and shook his head. "You cheated me after all."

"You cheated yourself, Martin. And now you're going to ride That Hell-Bound Train."

He pushed Martin up the steps and into the car ahead. As he entered, the train began to move and the whistle screamed. And Martin stood there in the swaying Pullman, gazing down the aisle at the other passengers. He could see them sitting there, and somehow it didn't seem strange at all.

Here they were: the drunks and the sinners, the gambling men and the grifters, the big-time spenders, the skirt chasers, and all the jolly crew. They knew where they were going, of course, but they didn't seem to be particularly concerned at the moment. The blinds were drawn on the windows, yet it was light inside, and they were all sitting around and singing and passing the bottle and laughing it up, telling their jokes and bragging their brags, just the way Daddy used to sing about them in the old song.

"Mighty nice traveling companions," Martin said. "Why, I've never seen such a pleasant bunch of people. I mean, they seem to be really enjoying themselves!"

"Sorry," the conductor told him. "I'm afraid things may not be quite so enjoyable once we pull into that Depot Way Down Yonder."

For the third time, he held out his hand. "Now, before you sit down, if you'll just give me that watch. I mean, a bargain's a bargain—"

Martin smiled. "A bargain's a bargain," he echoed. "I agreed to ride your train if I could stop Time when I found the right moment of happiness. So, if you don't mind, I think I'll just make certain adjustments."

Very slowly, Martin twisted the silver watch stem.

"No!" gasped the conductor. "No!"

But the watch stem turned.

"Do you realize what you've done?" the conductor panted. "Now we'll never reach the Depot. We'll just go on riding, all of us, forever and ever!"

Martin grinned. "I know," he said. "But the fun is in the trip, not the destination. You taught me that. And I'm looking forward to a wonderful trip."

The conductor groaned. "All right," he sighed, at last. "You got the best of me, after all. But when I think of spending eternity trapped here riding this train—"

"Cheer up!" Martin told him. "It won't be that bad. Looks like we have plenty to eat and drink. And after all, these are *your* kind of folks."

"But I'm the conductor! Think of the endless work this means for me!"

"Don't let it worry you," Martin said. "Look, maybe I can even help. If you were to find me another one of those caps, now, and let me keep this watch—"

And that's the way it finally worked out. Wearing his cap and silver watch, there's no happier person in or out of this world—now and forever—than Martin. Martin, the new brakeman on That Hell-Bound Train.

SENIOR HIGH LIBRARY
LEAVENWORTH, KANSAS

SC
80
HOK

Hoke, Helen
Horrifying and
hideous hauntings

DATE		
NOV 3 1987		
FEB 10 1989		

044758

© THE BAKER & TAYLOR CO.